19

THE ORCHARD BOOK OF
HEROES
— AND —
VILLAINS

For Inspector Coffey – we still think the world of you!
T.B.

To dear friends, Arlene and Tony, Jan and Paul
T.R.

Tony Bradman would like to thank Arts Council England for their support
while he was writing this book, and in particular Charles Beckett.

ORCHARD BOOKS
338 Euston Road, London NW1 3BH
Orchard Books Australia
Level 17-207 Kent Street, Sydney, NSW 2000

First published by Orchard Books in 2008

Text © Tony Bradman 2008
Illustrations © Tony Ross 2008

The rights of Tony Bradman to be identified as the author and
Tony Ross to be identified as the illustrator of this work
have been asserted by them in accordance with the
Copyright, Designs and Patents Act, 1988.

A CIP catalogue record for this book is available from the British Library.

ISBN 978 1 84362 973 3

1 3 5 7 9 10 8 6 4 2

Printed in China

Orchard Books is a division of Hachette Children's Books,
an Hachette Livre UK company.

THE ORCHARD BOOK OF
HEROES
— AND —
VILLAINS

TONY BRADMAN & TONY ROSS

ORCHARD BOOKS

CONTENTS

THE HIDEOUS ONE-EYED GIANT

THE STORY OF ODYSSEUS AND THE CYCLOPS

ODYSSEUS STOOD IN THE PROW OF HIS SHIP and peered into the thick sea fog before him. It was night, and though a full moon rode high in the sky above, its ghostly, silver light only broke through the murk from time to time. So he had no way of telling what lay ahead, no way at all.

Odysseus sighed. The night was windless, and the sail hung limp on the tall mast. He could hear the creaking of the oars, and soft splashes as the blades dipped in and out of the dark water. His crew were at their rowing benches, and he knew that each man trusted him to get them home. But Odysseus was beginning to wonder if he ever would.

He wanted to return to Greece as much as his warriors. It was ten years since he had seen his wife and son, ten years of hard fighting, of blood and death beneath the walls of Troy. He and his warriors – and the rest of the Greek army – would still be stuck there if he hadn't come up with the Wooden Horse, his brilliant idea for slipping into the city and winning the war. But then people didn't call him Clever Odysseus for nothing.

Although being clever wasn't much help when the weather was against them, as it had been since they had left the smoking ruins of Troy months ago. By now all the other Greeks would be at home, Odysseus thought. And here he was, still wandering the lonely waves with his men…

Suddenly there was a loud crunching noise, and the ship juddered to a halt. Several warriors fell off their benches, and for a moment there was utter panic. Odysseus held on and looked down, worried the ship might have hit some rocks. But all he saw was the sea foaming on sand.

"Relax, everybody," said Odysseus. "I think we've reached land."

"At last!" said a warrior. "Do you know where we are, my lord?"

"Not yet…" murmured Odysseus. Just then a breath of wind parted the fog, and he saw that the ship had run aground on a wide beach with hills beyond it. "But I'm going to find out. We'll make camp here for the night, and have a proper look round in the morning. Jump to it, lads."

When dawn came, the fog had gone and the sun shone in the sky.

"Right, time to do some exploring," said Odysseus. "I want twelve men to come with me. The rest of you are to stay here and guard the ship. We'll take something to eat and drink in case we're gone a long time."

"Er…there's not much left, my lord," said one of the men. "In fact, we don't have any food to speak of. We've got no water, either, only wine."

"Oh well, that will have to do," said Odysseus. Each of his men picked up a goatskin of wine. "I'll see about finding some fresh supplies too."

He strode off across the beach and the twelve men followed. Odysseus noticed that the hillside beyond was dotted with large caves. He and his men carefully crept towards the entrance of the nearest one.

"It looks like we've struck lucky, lads…" he said, and smiled.

He could hardly believe his eyes. A flock of sheep was penned in the cave, and its walls were lined with shelves, each stacked with rich sheep cheeses and large jars of cool, fresh ewe's milk. The men were delighted, and immediately started rounding up the sheep and grabbing the cheeses and jars. They wanted to take it all back to the ship as soon as possible.

"Whoa, hold on!" said Odysseus. "I think we'll wait for whoever lives here. I'm sure he'll let us have what we need. Besides, I want to talk to him and find out where we are. And how we get home from here."

The men weren't convinced. There was something about the place they didn't like, something rather strange and scary… But Odysseus said they could eat one of the sheep, and that persuaded them to stay.

In the middle of the cave were the ashes of a fire, and they quickly got it going again with some big chunks of wood they found. They sat round the leaping flames, gorging themselves on roasted meat for the first time in ages, eating cheese too, and swilling milk and laughing at each other's jokes.

After a while there was a terrific THUD! outside, and the cave floor trembled beneath them. The laughter slowly died in their mouths, and they glanced nervously at each other. There it was again...THUD! And again and again, THUD, THUD! Something was coming. The cave floor was shaking so much now that Odysseus and his warriors jumped to their feet. A moment later a shadow fell over the entrance, blocking out the light.

Odysseus looked up...
and gulped.

A colossal figure entered – a giant taller than ten men standing on each other's shoulders, a great bundle of uprooted trees under his arm. He was truly hideous. His mouth was full of teeth like moss-covered tombstones, and he had one enormous, evil eye in the middle of his forehead. He stared coldly at Odysseus and his men.

"Ah, strangers…" he growled, his voice like a slow rumble of thunder in the mountains. He let go of the trees, and they fell onto one of his great feet with a CRASH! He looked down and grimaced, then looked up at Odysseus again. "Who are you, and what are you doing in my cave?"

"We are simple Greeks, friend, on our way home from the Trojan War," said Odysseus, bravely stepping forward. Cowering in fear wouldn't get them anywhere, would it? Besides, the giant might be nicer than he looked. "But we got lost, as sailors sometimes do," he continued, "and we have come here to seek your help. Can you tell us where we are, exactly? Oh, and by the way, to whom do I have the pleasure of speaking?"

"This is the Land of the Cyclopes, and I am…" he paused, confusion passing across his face. Odysseus realised the giant was having trouble remembering his own name. "Er…Polyphemus," said the giant at last. "You seem to have helped yourself already. Was that one of my sheep?"

"Well, yes, actually, it was," said Odysseus, thinking fast. This wasn't good news. He had heard some very unpleasant things about the Cyclopes, and he knew that he would have to be careful with this Polyphemus. The giant probably had friends nearby too, which might be a problem. Still, at least Polyphemus didn't seem terribly bright – and that might work in their favour. "I'm sorry," Odysseus said. "We ran out of food on our voyage, and we were hungry. Perhaps we can repay you somehow."

"Oh, I'm sure you can," rumbled Polyphemus, grinning horribly. Then he reached out with his huge hands and grabbed a couple of warriors. He was very quick for a creature so enormous, and they had no chance of escape. "These two will do nicely in exchange," he said, chuckling as they struggled. "I've been wondering all day what to have for my supper."

He bit their heads off, and devoured them with a lot of eye-rolling and grunting and lip-smacking and drooling. Odysseus was horrified, and his men screamed. But there was nothing they could do. The giant was far too powerful for them to tackle, even with their sharp bronze swords.

The giant finished his grisly main course, then had dessert – a couple of shelves of cheese and the contents of several milk jars. After that he built up the fire with some of the trees he'd brought, let slip a few huge, rumbling burps, and settled down to sleep. Although not before he had rolled an enormous boulder across the cave entrance, totally blocking it.

Odysseus stood looking at the snoring giant, rage boiling in his veins. The creature obviously felt he didn't have to worry that they might hurt him while he slept. "We'll see about that," Odysseus thought, whipping his sword from its scabbard. He tried to work out where he could plunge it into Polyphemus to be certain of killing him. But then he thought again, and put his sword away. He realised that if he succeeded, he and his men would never leave the monster's cave.

Only Polyphemus – or a giant as strong as him – could roll back the boulder that blocked the entrance.

So much for being clever, Odysseus brooded. His men would have been better off without him. All he'd done was get them lost and lead them into danger. Now two men were dead, and he and the rest were doomed to the same gruesome fate. If only he could do something!

Odysseus racked his brains, desperately scanning the cave for inspiration. There was the snoring Polyphemus, his enormous eye closed. There was the fire, the bright flames leaping and casting dancing shadows on the cave walls. There were the trees stacked beside it, ready to be burned. And there on the cave floor were the goatskins of wine they had brought from the ship. And suddenly Odysseus knew what to do.

"OK, lads," he said. "We're getting out of here, and this is how…"

The next morning, Polyphemus woke up, stretched and, to Odysseus's dismay, breakfasted on another two warriors. Then the giant moved the boulder blocking the entrance and led out his flock. "See you later, strangers," he growled. "At supper time." He roared with laughter and rolled the boulder back with a BANG! making sure they couldn't escape.

Odysseus gritted his teeth, and quickly gave his orders. Using their bronze daggers, his men stripped the branches off the straightest of the trees until it was as smooth as the mast on their ship. Odysseus himself sharpened one end into a wicked point, and told his men to hold it in the fire until it was iron-hard. Finally he got them to hide it in the shadows where the cave wall met the floor, along with the goatskins of wine.

The day passed slowly, but at last there was a great THUD, THUD! outside, and the cave floor shook beneath their feet. Seconds later the boulder moved, and the giant entered with his sheep, his hideous teeth bared in a huge, evil grin, and rolled the boulder back to seal the cave behind him, shutting them in. Odysseus ordered his men to scatter, but Polyphemus still managed to grab a couple and gobble them up.

Odysseus groaned inwardly, yet kept himself under control. The giant settled down to his dessert, just as he had done the night before. But when he reached for his first jar of milk, Odysseus moved out of the shadows.

"Hey, Polyphemus, you ugly brute," said Odysseus. "Try this instead."

Odysseus casually threw a goatskin of wine onto the cave floor. The giant picked it up, opened it, took a sniff...and drained it in one gulp.

"Umm, that was delicious," growled Polyphemus, licking his lips. "Got any more? Eating little people like you always makes me very thirsty."

"I might have," said Odysseus. "But what will you give me for it? How about letting us go and proving that you're not such a monster after all?"

"Just hand it over, stranger," said Polyphemus. "Then we'll see, OK?"

Odysseus nodded to his men, and they threw the other goatskins of wine down in front of the giant. He grinned, and turned to Odysseus.

"Why, thank you, little man," said the giant. "Now I'll make you a promise. But first I want to know your name. I did tell you mine."

Odysseus frowned. He had learned long ago that it wasn't always a good idea to give your name to an enemy. He thought for a second, and then he smiled. The perfect false name had just popped into his mind. He had a feeling that Polyphemus was stupid enough to fall for it too.

"As you wish," said Odysseus. "My name is, of course...Nobody."

"Well then, Nobody…" said the giant, grinning at him. Odysseus could tell that he was completely fooled. "I promise…I'll eat you last."

Polyphemus roared with laughter at his own joke, and made a start on the rest of the wine. Odysseus rejoined his men and they huddled in the shadows, watching and waiting. Polyphemus swigged and burped, and before too long he was very, very drunk. At last he keeled over with a great CRASH! and the cave floor shook as if they were in an earthquake. The giant lay on his side, the rumble of his snores echoing from the walls.

"Quick, lads," Odysseus whispered eagerly. "This is our chance!"

The wine had done its work. Odysseus could be sure now the giant would stay asleep while they got ready. His men swung into action, picking up the sharpened tree and hurrying to the fire, straining under its weight now there were only six of them left. They placed the point in the flames again, but this time they kept it there till it was red-hot. Then Odysseus led them over to Polyphemus, who was lying with his head turned towards them, his eye closed, his eyelid fluttering.

"I'll bet he's having a lovely dream," whispered Odysseus. "Well, this is where we turn it into a nightmare. OK, lads, you know what to do!"

The remaining warriors grinned at him. They took aim, and swung the tree once, twice, three times…then plunged it through the giant's eyelid and into his single eyeball. Thick blood spurted, and there was a terrific sound of hissing and sizzling as the red-hot wood melted giant flesh. The warriors pushed with all their strength, and Odysseus joined in to help.

Polyphemus screamed in agony, leaped to his feet, and pulled the tree from his eye, more blood streaming down his face. He hurled the tree at the wall and crashed around, roaring and yelling at the top of his voice. Odysseus signalled to his men to keep out of the giant's way, and to stay silent. They huddled in the shadows at the back of the cave, and waited.

After a while, there was a THUD, THUD, THUD! outside, and the boulder covering the entrance was rolled back. Three colossal giants stood there, each of them even bigger and uglier than Polyphemus.

"Hey, what's all the noise, Polyphemus?" grumbled the biggest and ugliest. "Anyone would think you were being murdered or something."

"But I am, I am!" groaned Polyphemus. "He's trying to kill me, the evil little swine! Look, you idiots, can't you see? He's just put my eye out!"

"Er…who are you talking about?" said another of the three giants, and they peered in. Odysseus and his men shrank further into the shadows.

"Nobody!" Polyphemus yelled angrily. "Nobody is trying to kill me…"

Then he started banging his head against the cave wall in temper. The other three giants glanced at each other, and raised their single eyebrows.

"He always was a bit strange," said the one who hadn't spoken yet.

"And pretty stupid," said the one who'd spoken second. The other two nodded in agreement. "Now he's started to see ghosts and hurt himself."

"Well, I think we should leave him to stew in his own juice," muttered the one who'd spoken first. "Just keep the noise down, Polyphemus, OK?"

And with that, they turned and left, the great THUD, THUD, THUD of their footsteps fading into the distance. Odysseus couldn't help smiling at the way his clever name trick had worked. They weren't safe yet, though. They still had to get out of the cave without being caught by Polyphemus. For a brief instant Odysseus thought they would simply be able to make a dash for the mouth of the cave. Then Polyphemus sat down right by it.

"You won't get away, Nobody…" he muttered. "I'll eat you yet."

Odysseus frowned, and his men groaned. They could see the daylight outside, the clear, blue sky with its promise of life. But how could they get past the giant's great, groping hands? It seemed impossible. Odysseus, however, refused to admit defeat. He scanned the cave once more – and this time his eyes fell on the giant's sheep standing quietly in their pen.

There were some big rams in the flock, rams with thick, curly fleeces…

Suddenly Odysseus had another idea. He gathered his remaining men together and whispered his plan to them. Each man was to find a big ram and hold onto it underneath. Once they were in place, Odysseus would throw open the pen and shoo the flock out, then grab a ram himself.

And that's exactly what they did. Odysseus clung to the ram's belly, his face pressed into its smelly fleece, hoping the giant wouldn't see him.

"Ah, what's that?" said Polyphemus. "I hear something moving... But it's only my lovely sheep going out to graze in the pasture. Still, I'd better check that little swine, Nobody, and his pals aren't hiding among them."

Odysseus peeked from under his ram and saw Polyphemus running his great, meaty fingers over the backs of the bleating animals as they surged and jostled past him. The giant missed all the warriors hiding beneath.

Then it was the turn of Odysseus's ram, and he held his breath as the shadow of the giant's hand fell across him. "Umm, not there..." muttered Polyphemus. "If only I could find Nobody. I'd soon bash his brains out and rip him limb from limb! Oh well, off you go, my sweet flock. I'll come and round you up later. Er... if I can find you now that I'm blind. Oh, I curse the day when that evil little creature came to my cave..."

The ram trotted on, and Odysseus breathed again. As soon as he was a safe distance from the cave, he released his hold on the animal and stood up in the sun, free from the dark cave at last. His men were waiting, and they hurried to the beach, driving the giant's flock before them. The rest of the crew had almost given them up for dead, and were overjoyed they had returned. Odysseus told them what had happened, and they grieved for the friends they had lost. But they didn't have time to hang around.

"Right, let's get out of here," said Odysseus, and within a few moments the ship was heading away from the land, the men straining at their oars with all their strength, the sail beginning to fill with a light breeze. They hadn't gone very far when Odysseus turned to look at the beach, and saw a familiar figure looming high above the trees beyond the shore – the blind Polyphemus blundering around, searching for his precious flock.

"Hey, Polyphemus!" Odysseus shouted. "It's no good looking for your sheep – Nobody's got them! And they're going to make a fine supper!"

The crew laughed, and yelled insults at the giant. He heard, and yelled back and shook his fist. Then he picked up a huge rock from the beach and threw it in their direction.

It whistled through the air and plunged into the sea behind the stern with an enormous SPLASH! making a wave that picked up the ship…but only carried it further towards the open sea.

Odysseus knew they were safe for the time being. He also knew that whatever happened, whatever strange creatures they might encounter and adventures they might face, he would be clever enough to deal with them. He stood tall in the prow of his ship, longing to be at home, but sure now that he would get there someday. He looked ahead…

And saw that the sun had laid a path for him across the waves.

SHIPWRECKED!
THE STORY OF ROBINSON CRUSOE, CASTAWAY

YOUNG ROBINSON CRUSOE WAS A WILD LAD, the kind of boy who never did what he was told, and never listened to his father's advice. He thought his dad was just so…boring. Besides, what had Mr Crusoe Senior got to show for years of hard work and going without? A little money in the bank and a little house, that's what. Oh, and loads of daft sayings that he believed were the last word in wisdom. Stuff like "If a job's worth doing, Son, it's worth doing well" and "A place for everything, and everything in its place" and even "Where there's life, there's hope", for heaven's sake.

None of it made any sense to Robinson, and he spent a lot of time dreaming about the much more exciting life he was determined to have, one of travel and adventure and riches. He also spent a lot of time trying to avoid the chores his father insisted on giving him. But Mr Crusoe was equally determined to make young Robinson do them. So as you can imagine, there were plenty of arguments in the Crusoe household.

Finally Robinson could stand it no more, so he set off to seek his fortune. He joined the crew of a ship, and didn't look back once.

Things didn't turn out as he'd planned, though. Robinson worked as a sailor, then he became a trader, and eventually he bought a farm in South America. But it was a topsy-turvy life, and he was never satisfied. He certainly wasn't becoming wealthy as quickly as he had expected.

Then a chance came up for him to join a ship trading in the Caribbean. Robinson sold his farm and used all the money to buy goods to sell. He had them loaded aboard, and the ship left early one summer morning. The turquoise sea shimmered in the sunlight, a soft breeze filled the sails, and Robinson breathed in the salt air, sure that his luck had changed.

It had, but only for the worse. On the second day of the voyage, a wild hurricane blew out of the Atlantic, and the howling winds quickly drove the ship so far off course, the captain had no idea where they were. The sails were ripped from the spars, and the ship was tossed like a toy on colossal waves. Robinson felt horribly sick, and grimly held onto a mast.

Suddenly there was a CRASH! and the ship juddered to a halt, its masts swaying, its timbers groaning as if the vessel was in agony. By now it was night, and the winds were wilder than ever.

"We've struck a reef!" yelled the captain at last. "We're stuck on it too, and the sea will soon smash the hull to pieces... ABANDON SHIP!"

The crew wrestled the lifeboat into the sea, and they all jumped into it. They rowed away, hoping to find land. But the sea had other plans, and before long a giant wave

swamped them. Robinson fell into the foaming sea and felt himself being sucked down. He held his breath till he thought his lungs would burst. Then he was driven back to the surface, and the sea dumped him on a beach, the waves hissing and bubbling as they retreated. He turned round and saw another giant wave heading straight for him…

Three times the terrible sea caught him, even though he tried his best to outrun it, and three times it swallowed him and spat him out, but always further and further up the beach. At last it left him alone, and he crawled painfully into the shelter of some palm trees. The storm was still raging beyond the reef, the winds howling, the waves crashing on the sand.

It was quieter beneath the palm trees, but Robinson soon began to feel uneasy. Behind the palms there was jungle too thick for the moonlight to penetrate, a tangle of darkness. Maybe it was full of savage beasts that would like nothing more than a poor castaway for a tasty midnight snack. Robinson felt his heart pounding, and he scrambled up a tree. He sat on a branch with his back against the trunk, and tried to sleep.

He woke to the sounds of the sea sighing and birds squawking. He climbed down from the tree and slowly walked back onto the beach, stretching and feeling the aches and pains in his body from his battle with the waves. But the storm was over, the lagoon inside the reef dead calm now and the sky a washed-out grey. Robinson couldn't see the reef itself because of the morning mist rolling in over it from the sea beyond.

He stood there for a moment, wondering what had happened to his shipmates. Then he caught sight of an object lying half-buried in the sand nearby. It was the captain's hat. He soon found another hat, and then a couple of shoes that didn't match. But otherwise the beach was empty, and he began to realise that he might be the only survivor.

Robinson sat down heavily and covered his face with his hands. He was shipwrecked on a desert island, and he was alone. He felt desolate, and tearful at the thought of how very close he had come to death.

After a while he looked up again and noticed the mist was clearing. There was a shadow on the reef, and as the light grew stronger, Robinson saw something that gave him hope – the ship! He got to his feet and stared at it, amazed. The captain had been wrong. The sea hadn't smashed it to pieces at all. It was whole, although it was leaning at a crazy angle.

How awful, thought Robinson. Everyone would probably have survived if they'd stayed on board, although maybe some of the crew had made it back to the ship after the lifeboat had been overturned. There was only one way to find out. Robinson swam out across the lagoon. The water was warm and soothing, and it didn't take him too long to reach the reef.

He found a rope dangling from the bows, and used it to haul himself onto the ship. He stood there, water dripping from him onto the tilted deck.

"Ahoy, shipmates!" he called out at last. "Is there anyone aboard?"

There was no reply, only the sound of a soft breeze whispering in the rigging, the creaking of the vessel's timbers, the sea lapping at the hull.

Robinson went below decks to search the cabins, and heard a strange noise coming from inside one. He pulled the door open, and two small shapes dashed out between his feet, tripping him up, and a third, bigger, creature jumped on top of him. For a brief instant Robinson panicked.

Then he felt a large, wet tongue scraping at his face, and a pair of soft, small heads nuzzling against him, and he knew who these creatures were. It was Toby, the captain's dog, and the ship's cats, a young, white female called Freckles, and an old, ginger tom called Rufus.

"All right, Toby," said Robinson, laughing and trying to push the dog down. "You can stop licking me now. I gather you're all pleased to see me. Well, I'm pleased to see you three too."

Robinson returned to the top deck, the animals following him. He leaned against the mainmast and looked back at the island. He realised now it was quite small, its geography clear in the bright morning sun – the long, curved, yellow beach, the dense jungle dark behind it. A steep, rocky hill rose above both, its slopes mostly bare of vegetation.

There was no sign of human habitation anywhere. "So, Toby, my old messmate," Robinson murmured, "it seems we're in a pretty lonely spot. What do you think I should do, then?" He glanced down at the dog, who was sitting beside him, head tipped to one side, a quizzical expression on his face. The cats were off sniffing around somewhere. "No ideas?" said Robinson. "Can't say I'm surprised. All you're probably interested in is where your next meal is coming from." Toby's ears instantly pricked up. "I have to say I'm feeling a little peckish myself," Robinson continued. "Let's see what we can find…"

There were plenty of supplies in the galley – ship's biscuit, salt pork, barrels of apples, kegs of ale, bottles of wine, even a small box of scraps for Toby and the cats. Robinson felt much better after a hearty meal, and ready to come up with a plan of action. He wasn't sure, but he thought the island wasn't near the main trading routes, so it might be a long time before another ship found him. He would have to survive until then – which meant making some kind of shelter and keeping himself fed.

So it was a tremendous stroke of luck that the ship hadn't sunk. The food on board would keep him going while he worked out what the island had to offer. And of course there were other things to be had on such a vessel – ropes and timber and canvas, tools and nails in the ship's carpenter's stores, even muskets and pistols, gunpowder and shot.

"In fact, there's just about everything I need, Toby," Robinson said. "But I doubt if it will be here tomorrow. I'm sure the ship will sink tonight. So the question is, how do I get as much as possible from the ship to the island?" He looked around the deck, noticed some spars that had fallen from a mast – and had an idea. "I know…I'll make a raft!"

Robinson lashed the spars and pieces of timber together with ropes from the rigging, and before long his raft was bobbing on the sea beside the ship. He loaded it with as much as he could – food, tools, canvas, guns, powder, although there was still an enormous amount of everything left – and soon he was ready to leave. Freckles and Rufus sat nervously on a barrel of flour, but Toby stayed on the ship, refusing to jump down.

"Come on, Toby!" laughed Robinson, preparing to shove off with a pole he'd made. "You'll be safe, I promise! Oh well, suit yourself."

Toby whined, then scrambled at last onto the gunwale and leaped into the sea with a huge SPLASH! Robinson tried to get him to climb onto the raft, but Toby didn't want to, and swam beside it all the way to the beach.

Robinson dragged the raft up the beach and unloaded his stores beyond the high water mark. He picked out a musket, then covered everything else with a spare sail weighed down with stones, just to be safe.

"Right, Toby," said Robinson. "Time to do some exploring, I think."

Robinson, Toby and the cats walked along the beach until they came to a stream that emerged from the jungle and flowed into the sea.

"Ah, fresh water," said Robinson, smiling. "That's good…"

The stream twisted and turned through the jungle and finally led to the rocky hill Robinson had seen from the ship. At the base of the hill was a clearing and the entrance to a small cave. The stream came from a spring that bubbled up from the ground nearby. Robinson realised this spot would make a perfect place to build his shelter.

Within a few hours he had taken all his stores to the cave, and used a spare sail to make an awning in front of it. He chopped down a couple of trees for firewood, sharpened the branches into stakes, and planted them in a semicircle round the edge of the clearing as a fence. It took him all afternoon, but it certainly made him feel a lot safer.

He lit a fire and sat beside it to eat his supper of ship's biscuit and salt pork, with Toby dozing beside him. Freckles and Rufus had found them, and lay cuddled up to each other and the dog. Robinson suddenly felt tired, and dozed off himself as the sun went down, although he didn't sleep well, his dreams full of winds and waves and fierce wild animals…

He woke early the next morning, his spirits low. He wanted to check on the ship but was sure it would be gone. He set off down the stream to the beach. Toby was excited and ran ahead, stopping every so often to sniff at plants. Before long they came to the raft, which was where they had left it the day before. Robinson turned and looked out at the calm sea – and there was the ship, still perched on the reef, still whole.

"Well I never," said Robinson. "Look at that, Toby. It didn't sink last night after all. Maybe I could get some more stuff off before it does."

He lost count of the number of trips he made from shore to ship and ship to shore, then back up the beach and through the jungle to his cave. It was hard work in the hot sun, but it gave him huge satisfaction to see his heap of supplies growing. He only stopped when the sun went down.

"Phew, what a day!" he said as he ate his evening meal. "But it was definitely worth it. If nothing else, at least we've got some light now!"

Robinson had found a dozen candles in the captain's cabin, and now one lit the inside of his cave with a cosy golden glow. He was beginning to feel relaxed for the first time since the shipwreck. And when he slept that night, he dreamed only of what he was going to do with his stores.

The next day, Robinson discovered to his delight that the ship still hadn't sunk. That gave him the chance to make more trips on the raft to it, and to bring away more stuff that might be useful. The ship was there the next day, and the day after that, and the day after, and Robinson slipped into a busy routine of trips to the ship and work on his shelter.

He spent part of each day sorting his booty and storing it away properly in the cave. He also improved his shelter, raising the fence and making a ladder to get in and out, and building a kind of big, wooden porch for the cave entrance with timber from the ship. And in between doing all that, he and Toby explored as much of the island as possible.

"I think we're going to be fine, Toby," Robinson said as they were heading home late one afternoon. It was the twelfth day since the wreck. "It's not such a scary place as I thought. There aren't any dangerous wild animals here, just lots of goats, and I can hunt them for meat. I might even be able to catch a few and keep them for their milk. And there are fish in the lagoon, so Freckles and Rufus can have the occasional treat."

That evening, Robinson sat in his cave surrounded by his supplies in their neat piles, his tools and weapons all neatly arranged too. He frowned, a memory nagging somewhere at the back of his mind. And then it came to him, and he found himself thinking about his father.

"A place for everything, and everything in its place," Robinson said, and smiled. "I think Dad would be impressed, Toby," he said. "And what was that other thing he used to say? Oh yes, 'If a job's worth doing, it's worth doing well.' Do you know, I can see the point of that now. I've done a pretty good job of stripping the ship of anything that might be useful, but there's still plenty aboard. So I'll keep going until the job is done." Robinson lay down, his head full of plans, and quickly fell asleep. He didn't sleep for long, though. Ever since the shipwreck, the weather had been hot and sunny, the blue sky cloudless every day. But that night there was a great storm. Robinson huddled in his cave with Toby and Freckles and Rufus, all of them jumping when the thunder went…BOOM! and listening to the wild winds howling and thrashing through the jungle.

The storm ended at dawn, and Robinson set off with Toby to see what it had done to the island. The jungle looked rather battered, and lots of broken branches were strewn across the beach. As Robinson walked along, he remembered that this was his thirteenth day as a castaway.

Then he looked out to the reef, and saw that the ship had vanished.

He couldn't believe it at first, and peered into the distance, sheltering his eyes from the glare of the morning sun, searching for the familiar, reassuring shape. But there was no doubt it was gone. Robinson's heart sank, and the good mood and confidence of the last few days crumbled.

He turned around and walked away, his head down, stumbling into the jungle. Then he started running, Toby barking at his heels. Robinson ran and ran and ran, crashing through the branches and undergrowth, and after a while he realised he was heading upwards, the ground rising beneath his feet. Soon he found himself at the top of the rocky hill.

From there he could have seen the whole island, the dark blue sea surrounding it calm and flat again now after the storm, glittering under the hot sun and stretching to the far horizon. But his eyes were full of tears, and for a time he could see nothing. He felt Toby gently nudge his leg, and the dog whined, confused and worried about his master.

Until that morning, Robinson hadn't realised that the ship hadn't just been a source of supplies. In his mind it had been a kind of link with the outside world, a talisman,

proof somehow that one day another ship would come along and rescue him. Now he felt more alone than he had ever done before, and it was as if his soul had filled with darkness.

What point was there in everything he'd done since the shipwreck? It was all such a waste of time. There was probably nothing ahead of him but years of solitude and hardship and struggle, and finally a sad, lonely death. There wouldn't even be anybody around to bury him. He might as well save himself the bother and simply jump off the nearest cliff.

There was a steep drop in front of him, and he moved towards it. He closed his eyes, felt the wind tug at him –

and suddenly he remembered something else his father used to say. It was almost as if he could hear his father's voice speaking inside his head. "Where there's life, there's hope…"

"You were right, Dad," Robinson murmured, suddenly understanding. He opened his eyes, looked down at Toby, and fondled the dog's ears. "For all we know, Toby, a ship might turn up tomorrow," he said. "And if I'm dead, I won't be here to greet it, will I? No, I'm alive, and I think I'd like to stay that way. Come on, let's go home. I've still got chores to do. Hey, did I say chores?" he laughed. "If only Dad could see me now!" Robinson strode off, Toby running along beside him, happy to see his master smiling again.

There was no ship the next day, or the day after that, or the day after that. In fact, it was many years before Robinson was rescued, and there were many more dark moments before that day. But Robinson never, ever gave up hope, and that's what made him a hero.

Not the kind of hero who does daring deeds and has great adventures seeking glory, of course. Robinson Crusoe was a quiet hero, a bit like his father – a man who took what life dealt him, and did the best he could.

And sometimes that's just about the hardest kind of hero to be.

TERROR IN THE NIGHT

THE STORY OF BEOWULF THE HERO

LONG AGO, IN THE FAR-OFF DAYS OF LEGEND, when being a hero still counted for something in the cold, hard lands of the north, a young warrior called Beowulf heard a tale that set his mind racing with dreams of glory.

One night, a monster called Grendel had crept into the hall of a Danish chieftain by the name of Rothgar. The monster killed many of Rothgar's warriors, and left nothing but their blood splattered on the walls. Grendel had returned the next night, and every night since. So Rothgar had to leave his hall empty in the sunless hours, and his people lived in terror.

It was said that no one could stand up to Grendel and survive, although many mighty warriors had tried their hands against him. That made it even more tempting for Beowulf to take on the challenge himself. He was already known here and there in the north for his great strength. But this was the perfect chance for him to show what he could really do.

"Imagine how famous I would be if I managed to kill the monster," he thought. "It would be enough to make me a great hero…and harpists would sing about my exploits for thousands of years to come."

Beowulf soon set sail for Denmark, taking with him the band of young warriors he often led into battle. A week or so later, he and his shield-brothers marched through Rothgar's village, the northern sunlight glinting on their helmets and mailshirts, their sharp swords and spears.

Rothgar was sitting at the far end of his hall, deep in moody thought, his face clouded. A few of his warriors were standing nearby. Beowulf strode up to him, past heaps of smashed tables and benches, all marked with gouges and scratches. Bloodstains covered the walls, and there was no bright, warming fire burning in the dead hearth, only cold, grey ashes.

"Hail, Rothgar," said Beowulf. "I've come to solve your problem."

"Is that so?" said one of Rothgar's men, looking Beowulf up and down. The man obviously wasn't that impressed. "Well then, who are you?"

"My name is Beowulf, and these are my shield-brothers," the young warrior said, returning the man's stare. "And who might you be, friend?"

The man didn't bother to reply, but turned to Rothgar instead. "Don't listen to him, my lord," he said. "He can't help us. He's like all the others. Full of boasting, I'll bet, but no real match for a monster like Grendel."

"You're probably right, Unferth," said Rothgar. "But I think I've heard his name before. You've gained something of a reputation, Beowulf."

"True," said Beowulf, standing tall and proud before the chieftain. "So I hope that means you'll allow me to take on this evil creature for you."

"Don't ask me that…" said Rothgar. "I would hate to see yet another young warrior slaughtered. What do you know about Grendel, anyway?"

"Not much," said Beowulf, shrugging. "Except that he haunts your hall at night, and has killed a lot of warriors. What else is there to know?"

"A great deal," said Unferth. "Grendel is strong and cunning and shows no mercy. When he chooses, he is harder to see than the shadow of a shadow. He finds ways in, where no creature of daylight could go…"

"And it also seems that no blade made by humans can harm him, nor even make a mark on his scaly hide," Rothgar muttered. "Some believe that he lives in a lake in the marshes with his mother, another creature of darkness and pure evil. So, young man – what do you say now?"

Beowulf hesitated. The truth was that he had begun to feel nervous. He hadn't fully understood just what a challenge Grendel might be till then – a straight fight was one thing, but grappling with the monster they had just described…well, that was different. But Beowulf kept an iron grip on himself, determined not to show what he was feeling inside. He hadn't come all this way only to give up at the first touch of fear.

"Exactly the same," he replied. "I'm here to rid you of this evil, and in front of every man present I swear that's what I will do. Or die trying."

Rothgar smiled, and his men seemed impressed – even Unferth.

"Very well," said Rothgar. "Tonight you will face the monster as you wish. And if you defeat him, I will reward you handsomely. But first let me feed you and your men. We still know how to treat guests here."

Rothgar told his men to clear up the hall as best they could, and get a fire going, and before long a marvellous feast was laid on for Beowulf and his men. Rothgar's wife came to meet them, and laughter echoed in the rafters, something that hadn't been heard there for a very long time. But through the open doorway, Beowulf could see the daylight fading. Night was coming, and he knew Grendel wouldn't be far behind.

Soon the feast was over, and the moment came for Rothgar and his wife and men to leave the hall. Rothgar wished Beowulf luck. He gripped his hand and talked of the gold and jewels and fine weapons and horses he would give him – if the young warrior survived the night. But Beowulf could see in Rothgar's sad eyes that the chieftain didn't think he would…

"I won't be needing this," Beowulf said, giving his sword to one of his shield-brothers for safekeeping. He positioned them round the hall, and took a spot right in the middle, by the fire. He ordered his men to tell him as soon as they heard or saw anything, and then he would step forward to fight Grendel with his bare hands. That was the plan, at any rate. He had done plenty of wrestling in his time, and had beaten many strong men.

They settled down to wait, the darkness in the doorway deepening. Beowulf sat by the flickering firelight, the flames shrinking, the shadows in the corners of the hall lengthening and flowing into each other. One by one, Beowulf's men fell asleep, their chins nodding onto their chests. But Beowulf stayed awake. Then his eyelids began to grow heavy too.

All at once, the monster, Grendel, exploded out of the darkness, hissing and spitting and slashing at Beowulf with his sharp, curved talons. The young warrior was knocked off his feet, crashing into the hearth and sending a shower of sparks flying, although he still managed to hold back the monster. Beowulf was on his back now with Grendel on top of him, the monster snarling and snapping and trying to rip out his throat.

Grendel stank of the marshes, and was slimy to the touch. He was incredibly strong too, exactly as Unferth had said. He pressed down on Beowulf, his foul breath beating into the young warrior's face, drool dripping from his pointed, yellow fangs. Beowulf resisted with all his might, and slowly began to force Grendel back. He heard his shield-brothers shouting, and suddenly a torch flared into life, then another.

Beowulf could see his opponent now, the thick, scaly, grey hide, the body like a man's, although much bigger and rippling with muscle. The young warrior rolled to one side, holding the monster's wrists and trying to get on top of him. Soon they were on their knees, then on their feet, neither of them willing to let go, the terrible struggle continuing.

Monster and man stared at each other, their faces almost touching. Beowulf's men hacked at Grendel with their swords, but he seemed not to notice. He started pressing Beowulf down once more, torchlight glinting in his black eyes. His mouth widened in a wicked smile, and those yellow fangs came closer and closer to the soft flesh of Beowulf's throat...

Beowulf summoned up all his massive strength. He squeezed the monster's wrists and pushed back at him again – and gradually he began to win. "You've met your match at last, Grendel..." he muttered from between gritted teeth, and the monster's smile faded. Soon Beowulf could see fear in the monster's eyes, and feel him trying to pull away.

Eventually Beowulf pinned Grendel down, and secured both of the monster's wrists in one mighty hand. Then with the other he reached for Grendel's throat. Strangling would probably be the best way to kill him.

Grendel squealed in panic, freed one arm and desperately tried to escape. Beowulf held on grimly, and warrior and monster crashed round the hall, smashing into the walls and knocking over Beowulf's men like so many skittles. At last there was a great sound of flesh tearing and bones cracking, and the monster fled, howling, into the night, leaving Beowulf holding a strange and grisly trophy – Grendel's other arm and shoulder.

Beowulf nailed it to a beam, and his men cheered him to the rafters.

In the morning, when Rothgar returned to his hall, he was amazed to see Grendel's arm. Of course he was also delighted that Beowulf had lived to tell the incredible tale of what had happened. And he was even more delighted with the news that Unferth brought him soon after.

"We followed Grendel's trail all the way to the lake in the marshes, my lord," said Unferth. "That's where it stops. The monster must have been returning to his lair. And the water is stained red with his blood."

"He couldn't possibly have survived such a wound…" said Rothgar. "Which means, Beowulf, that you are the greatest hero of our time!"

The young warrior grinned as everyone cheered again. Then Rothgar laid on an even more magnificent feast, and brought out wonderful gifts for Beowulf and his men – all the fine things he had talked of, and lots more besides. Beowulf ate and drank and listened to the harpist singing, hardly able to believe that his exploits were the subject of the song.

That night, as he finally lay down to rest in Rothgar's hall along with everyone else, he felt utterly exhausted. He was bruised and battered too, and he knew that it had been a desperately close-run contest. The monster had tested him to the very limits of his strength. Another moment or two and one of his arms might have been ripped out, not Grendel's.

"Well, thank goodness it's all over, anyway," thought Beowulf. He smiled as he remembered what Rothgar had said, and fell asleep…

But it wasn't over. He woke to the sound of screaming. People were running round in terror, their shadows dancing in the firelight. A huge shape snarled and slashed at anyone who was near, and finally vanished.

Torches flared, and Beowulf heard gasps, followed by howls of grief. He quickly pushed through the crowd and saw Rothgar by a pool of blood. A trail of red footprints led from it to the hall door. And Grendel's arm had gone, pulled down from the wall and carried off into the night.

"Grim news, Beowulf," said Rothgar, turning to him. "Death still stalks my hall. I've lost another brave warrior to a monster from the marsh."

"What, you mean that Grendel isn't dead?" said Beowulf.

"Oh, Grendel is dead, right enough," Rothgar muttered, his face grim. "The beast who came here tonight had both her arms… I had always thought the story about Grendel having a mother was a tale to frighten little children. But it's true, and she came to seek revenge for her son."

Then everybody in the hall started talking at once, their fear and horror making them loud. Before long they convinced themselves that Grendel's mother was impossibly strong and far more powerful than her son, and that she would return to hunt them each night, just as he had done.

"What shall we do?" somebody wailed at last. "We're all doomed!"

"Oh no, we're not!" somebody else yelled. "Beowulf will save us!"

"Yes, Beowulf!" the crowd yelled. They turned to the young warrior, and they started to chant his name. "Beowulf! BEOWULF! BEOWULF!"

"ENOUGH!" Rothgar shouted at last, and the hall fell silent. "No man should be forced to fight such a hellish creature," said Rothgar. "And if you choose not to, Beowulf, you can still leave here with the gifts I gave you, and feel no shame. You've done your share, and I thank you."

All eyes were on the young warrior now. Beowulf was silent, deep in thought, his head down. Then he looked up at Rothgar, and at Unferth.

"And what if there is another monster, after I kill this one?" he said.

"Beowulf, there is always another monster,"

42

Rothgar said. "Or armies of invaders, like hungry wolves in the winter, or other threats…"

And that's when Beowulf realised there was a lot more to this business of being a hero than he had thought. It seemed it wasn't just about glory, and harpists singing songs about your exploits. These people were relying on him. They had seen him take on one monster and win, and now they were expecting him to defeat a bigger, stronger, scarier opponent.

But what if he couldn't do it? Beowulf scanned the ring of faces before him, saw the hope and trust in their eyes – the belief that he would succeed again and save them. Suddenly all the fear inside him fell away. He knew he couldn't let these people down, even if it meant losing his life.

"So be it," he said, standing tall and proud. "I choose…to fight!"

A great roar went up in the hall,

and soon Beowulf and his shield-brothers were on the trail of Grendel's mother. Her huge footprints were plain to see beside the blood trail left by Grendel. Rothgar had promised Beowulf more fine gifts, but the only thing on Beowulf's mind was killing the monster. He didn't care any more if harpists sang about him afterwards.

They did, though. They sang of how Beowulf found a mist-covered lake in the marshes, of how he plunged deep beneath its tainted surface and tracked Grendel's mother to her cave, of how he fought a mighty fight with her over the body of her dead son – and of how he won. They sang of how he returned with the heads of both monsters, and left Rothgar and his people free forever from the terror that had haunted their nights.

And we still sing the same song today – that of Beowulf the hero!

DINOSAUR ENCOUNTER

THE STORY OF AXEL LIDENBROCK'S JOURNEY TO THE CENTRE OF THE EARTH

"OH, THERE YOU ARE, AXEL!" burbled an excited Professor Lidenbrock when his nephew came home from school one day. "I want you to go to your room this instant and pack your rucksack. We're taking a little trip."

"Oh no," thought Axel. "Where are we going this time?" His parents had died in an accident when he was small, and he had lived with his uncle for as long as he could remember. Certainly long enough to know that when the professor used a phrase such as 'a little trip' he didn't mean it in the same way as other people.

Professor Lidenbrock was what you might call eccentric. He was also the most brilliant scientist in their native Germany, if not the whole world. The professor was interested in everything, but he was especially fascinated by old rocks, an obsession Axel simply couldn't understand.

"And where exactly are we going?" said Axel, preparing himself for news of another boring expedition. The professor's 'little trips' usually involved journeys to distant places where there always seemed to be lots of mountains. Axel had seen enough mountains to last him a lifetime.

"You probably won't believe me when I tell you," said the professor, grinning at him like a little boy. "In fact, I can hardly believe it myself!"

Axel sighed. He loved his uncle, but getting information out of him sometimes seemed like getting blood out of a stone. Or even an old rock.

"OK, let me guess," said Axel. "We're off to a funfair, or a circus, or…"

"No, my dear boy!" said the professor, horrified, staring at him as if he'd gone mad. "We're going on a journey to…the centre of the Earth!"

Axel's jaw dropped, and his uncle explained. Through the study of ancient books and maps, Professor Lidenbrock had discovered a way to descend further below the Earth's surface than anyone before, and yes, perhaps even to the very centre of the planet. There was a route they could follow. But first it seemed they would have to go to Iceland.

"I might have known it would be somewhere in the north," muttered Axel, who didn't like the cold. "Do we have to do this, Uncle? I mean, it's all very interesting, but it sounds like it could be dangerous too."

"Oh, Axel!" said the professor, frowning. "Where's your sense of adventure? We might end up being the most famous explorers in history! And besides, think of all the amazing rocks we could find down there."

"Or we might end up dead," said Axel. "I know what you're like. You do things without thinking, and you've almost got yourself killed before."

There had been several occasions when the professor's enthusiasm had made him careless, and he had ignored Axel's warnings about things like a sheer drop on a mountain path, or the crumbling edge of a cliff. Axel had managed to save him so far, but there was no guarantee he would always be able to. He often found himself wishing the professor would take him more seriously. Or maybe even just listen to him occasionally.

The professor never had, though, and he obviously wasn't about to start now.

"Umm, I wonder if I might need my small microscope…" the professor was murmuring to himself. "Er…I'm sorry, Axel, what did you say?"

"Nothing, Uncle," said Axel, and sighed again. "I'll go and pack."

The very next day, they set sail from their home city of Hamburg on a ship bound for Iceland, and a week after that they arrived in the capital, Reykjavik. From there they hiked across a rocky landscape, heading for Snaefells, a great extinct volcano.

"Huh, it looks like another mountain to me," Axel muttered as they slogged up the slope towards the top. It was supposed to be spring, but the sky was grey and the wind was freezing.

At last they reached the summit, and climbed over the rim into the volcano's crater. In the middle was a large hole surrounded by rocks.

"Right, this is the place," said the professor. "At the bottom there should be a passageway that will lead us to where we want to go."

"Fine, but how do we get to it?" said Axel, nervously peering into a pool of deep blackness. "It doesn't look to me as if there is a bottom."

"Of course there is!" said the professor. "All we have to do is climb down." But then he frowned, and eased the straps of the big pack he had on his back. Axel had one too. "Mind you," muttered the professor, "that won't be easy with these ridiculously overstuffed rucksacks. I can't imagine why you insisted on us bringing so much stuff. Heaven knows how I'm going to find any space for the rock samples I intend to collect!"

Axel tutted as they started climbing down. They would be in big trouble if he'd left the packing to his uncle. The professor wasn't very practical, and had only thought about what scientific equipment he might need on the expedition. Axel had made sure they had plenty of food, as well as a change of clothes each, and a few other things that might come in handy, like lamps, ropes, a sharp knife and even a small tent.

They reached the bottom at last. The hole they'd come through was now a tiny circle of daylight far above them. Axel lit the lamps and gave one to his uncle, and they held them up, the golden glow pushing back the darkness. Axel saw that he and the professor were standing in a vast cavern, its flat, rocky floor dotted with lots more holes. Most were quite small, but some were large enough to swallow a fair-sized house.

"What are these, Uncle?" Axel said, peering down into the nearest one.

"They're lava shafts, my boy," said the professor. "When the volcano was active, boiling-hot lava would shoot up them from below."

"Really?" Axel said uneasily. "Er…that must have been quite a sight."

"Oh yes," the professor murmured absently. He was studying a map in the light of his lamp, and scanning the cavern's walls. "Some of them had a floor of solid rock, like a cap in a bottle. So anything sitting on top of that would have been blown well clear of the crater… Ah, there it is!" he suddenly exclaimed. "I knew it would be around here somewhere!"

The professor hurried over to a spot nearby, and Axel followed him. The light from their lamps revealed an opening in the cavern wall. A narrow tunnel appeared to slope downwards from it into deep gloom. Its sides and roof were rough and rocky, its floor smooth, like black marble.

"Wonderful! This is the passageway I was talking about, Axel," said the professor, his voice full of excitement. "Come on, let's get going!"

"Er…wait a minute, Uncle," said Axel, holding the professor back. "Are you sure it isn't dangerous? It looks a little, well…slippery to me."

"Don't be ridiculous, Axel," said the professor, striding off down the tunnel and pulling his nephew along behind him. "It's perfectly safe!"

Axel sighed…and gave in. They hadn't gone far, however, when he felt his feet sliding on the smooth rock, and he noticed the professor having the same problem. The slope grew steeper, and soon they were slipping and scrabbling to hold on to the sides of the tunnel. "Yikes, I can't stand up!" yelled the professor at last. He fell with a thump and knocked Axel over. Their lamps smashed into the sides of the tunnel and went out. They were left in profound darkness as they slid down faster and faster, screaming at the tops of their voices. The shaft seemed endless. But just when Axel thought he couldn't stand it any more, he shot out of the dark and into light. He spun head over heels through the air, and crashed onto a surface which yielded enough to break his fall. He rolled over several times before finally coming to rest flat on his face, all the breath knocked out of him.

49

He heard the professor land beside him, and for a few seconds the two of them lay there, unable to move or speak. Eventually Axel raised his head to look at his uncle, squinting and shielding his eyes from the light. To his surprise he saw that the professor was already getting to his feet.

"Are you all…" Axel started to say, but his voice slowly trailed away as he took in their surroundings. They appeared to have landed on a beach of fine, yellow sand. A calm, blue sea was lapping at its edge, and thick, green jungle stood behind it. There was a hazy light over the whole scene. "But…what…how…where on Earth are we?" Axel stammered.

"We're not anywhere on the Earth," said the professor. "We're definitely still inside it. And I don't know what this place is, unless…"

"What, Uncle?" said Axel, getting to his feet. The professor wasn't listening, of course. He was walking along the sand, his eyes raised.

Axel saw he was looking at a wall of rock that cut off one end of the beach. There was a hole in it a fair way up, and Axel realised it was the bottom of the shaft down which they had fallen. The wall of rock climbed high over their heads, curving steeply until it disappeared from view.

"I think this is an underground cavern," said the professor, "although obviously it's a big one. I'd guess it was miles across, and miles deep."

"But where did all this water come from?" said Axel. "I mean, it looks like an ocean. And what about the jungle? And why isn't it dark in here?"

Axel realised there was something strange about the light. It wasn't like sunshine. It was a steady, almost artificial, glow, with no warmth, and yet he didn't feel cold. There was a peculiar fuzziness high above them, a whiteness shot through with flickers and flashes of fire.

"Well, that's all fairly easy to explain," said the professor. "My guess would be that the water simply leaked from above, perhaps through a crack in the sea-bed – don't forget, we're probably below the Atlantic. And there are always plant seeds in any sea, washed into it by rivers…"

The professor rambled on for ages, describing how the crack in the sea-bed had probably closed up after a while, leaving the cavern sealed, except for the shaft they'd come down. He thought the light was the result of large, electrically-charged clouds forming under the roof of the cavern.

"So what are we going to do, Uncle?" Axel asked. "We can't go back the way we came. We'd never climb that shaft, not in a million years."

"Who said anything about going back?" replied the professor, beaming at him.

"No, my boy, we press on. I'll admit I wasn't expecting such an obstacle. This isn't the centre of the Earth, but I'm sure we're going in the right direction. We just have to think of a way to get across this sea."

"We'd have to build a boat, or a raft…" said Axel with a frown.

"What a splendid idea!" said the professor. "I suggest you make a start on that while I do a spot of exploring. This is just too good a chance to miss. Why, the rocks here must be fascinating, utterly fascinating…"

The professor scuttled off happily. Axel sighed, and started looking for the means to make a raft. It wasn't long before he had worked out what to do. Luckily there were quite a few fallen trees in the jungle, and he dragged a dozen of the smaller ones onto the beach, trimmed them with his sharp knife, and lashed them together with his ropes. He made a tiller to steer with, and a mast, and converted the tent into a sail. The professor returned a few hours later, delighted with the rocks he'd found.

"Not bad, though I do say so myself…" Axel murmured at last, smiling at his handiwork. "Are you ready, Uncle? I think we should get going."

But as usual, the professor wasn't listening. He was already sitting by the mast, studying his new-found treasures with a magnifying glass. Axel shrugged, and shoved off with a pole he'd cut from a branch. Soon the raft was moving along at quite a speed, a strong breeze filling the sail.

"I thought we'd head in a straight line," said Axel, who was doing the steering, of course. "I'm pretty sure I can see the far wall of the cavern." There was another steep wall of dark rock in the distance. "Hang on a second," he said, suddenly alert. "What's that strange noise?"

"Noise?" said the professor, looking up. "I don't hear anything."

"There it is again," said Axel. He could hear it more clearly now, a strange bellowing like a cow in pain, but a long way off to their right.

Just then he felt the raft begin to bob up and down, and he realised the sea had turned choppy, with lots of small waves following each other in quick succession. They came from the same direction as the noise.

"Umm, how interesting," murmured the professor, getting to his feet and peering across the water. "I think we need to investigate, Axel."

"Well, I don't, Uncle," Axel muttered. The noise made him feel quite nervous. "I'd much rather keep going. We have no idea what it could be."

"Exactly!" said the professor. "So we'd better find out. After all, we're here to discover things. And as I am the leader of our little expedition…"

Axel didn't reply. He simply sighed once more and – against his better judgement – swung the tiller over, changing their course. Soon the raft was breasting some quite large waves. The noise grew louder, and now Axel could hear growling, and what sounded like huge amounts of splashing too. Then it stopped, just as suddenly as it had begun.

The waves flattened, and the raft drifted for a while in silence, except for the gentle lapping of the water. Axel looked down and thought he saw a dark shape moving through the depths. But whatever it was…vanished.

"Oh well, never mind," the professor said cheerily, already turning back to his rocks. "It looks like we aren't going to find out what it—"

Suddenly a giant head burst from the water nearby, rising up and up and up on an impossibly long neck. Before they knew it, an enormous creature stared down at them, its huge body breaking through the waves like an island emerging from the sea. It had a vast mouth, with rows and rows of wickedly sharp teeth. They were clamped onto the body of something resembling a cross between a whale and a shark. Axel could see blood pouring from the captured beast, although it was twitching feebly.

"Er…any idea w-w-what these creatures are, Uncle?" Axel whispered, unable to take his eyes from them. The big one tipped its head to the side and seemed to return his gaze, narrowing its own surprisingly small eyes.

"Why, of course!" murmured the professor, a note of wonder in his voice. "Although I hardly imagined that I would ever encounter genuine, living examples. Animals like these have been extinct for millions of years on the surface of the Earth, Axel. You're looking at a plesiosaurus – that's the larger one – and an ichthyosaurus, both mighty denizens of the ancient oceans. In short, we have before us…a dinosaur and its prey!"

"That's terrific, Uncle," muttered Axel. The plesiosaurus bit a little harder on its prey, which bellowed in pain. "But I think we ought to get out of here. We seem to have interrupted the big one's lunch, and I wouldn't want it to start thinking of us as dessert."

"Don't be ridiculous, Axel," said the professor crossly. "This is a fantastic opportunity. I must make some notes, draw a sketch or two…"

Suddenly there was a dull boom of thunder high above, and those flickers and flashes of fire turned into streaks of lightning. A strong wind picked up, instantly filling the little raft's sail and pushing it away from the plesiosaurus, much to Axel's relief. The creature looked puzzled, and stared after them for a while. Then it seemed to make a decision. It swallowed the ichthyosaurus in one huge gulp…and came after the raft.

"Watch out, Uncle!" yelled Axel, swinging the tiller hard over. The plesiosaurus roared and snapped at them, but it just missed and plunged beneath the waves with a huge splash, drenching Axel and the professor.

"What are you playing at, Axel?" shouted the professor. "How can I possibly make a sketch if you're flinging the raft all over the place?"

"Sorry, Uncle!" yelled Axel, realising the plesiosaurus was getting ready for another lunge. "But I don't actually have much choice…"

Axel threw the tiller hard the other way, and the creature missed again, although it managed to get close enough for Axel to smell its foul, fishy breath and see just how sharp its teeth were. He had a feeling it wouldn't miss a third time…but luckily the wind was strengthening, and soon the raft was moving incredibly fast, riding the crest of some enormous waves.

All Axel could do now was hold on to stop himself being washed overboard in the storm, although their rucksacks and anything that wasn't tied down soon went. At least the professor had stopped complaining, and was grimly hanging onto the mast. Axel risked a peek behind, and saw the plesiosaurus give up, its long neck vanishing beneath the wild sea.

He turned to look ahead once more…and saw the cavern wall looming over them. Axel realised that if they hit it at the speed they were travelling they would never survive. He desperately tried to think of a way to slow the raft down, but it seemed impossible. Then he caught a glimpse of an opening in the rock, and swung the tiller hard over.

They swept onwards, riding the crest of the biggest wave yet, both of them screaming at the tops of their voices…and they plunged into the opening, which was just large enough to let them through. They landed with a CRASH! in the middle of a circular space not much bigger than the raft. Water swirled around them, then receded, hissing back out to sea.

"Phew, I really didn't think we were going to make it," Axel muttered, trying to get his breathing under control. At least they were safe for the time being. Or were they? He looked up, and although there wasn't much light coming in from outside, he realised they weren't in a cave – there was no rocky ceiling above them. The raft was at the bottom of a shaft which rose as far as Axel could see, its upper reaches lost in darkness.

"Where are we now, Uncle?" he said, beginning to feel nervous again.

"I'm not entirely sure, my boy," the professor said vaguely. There were several openings in the walls, large and small, and he was peering into one, although he was still standing on the raft. "But these rocks are amazing!" he said. "Help me climb up here, Axel, I need a closer look…"

"Er…no, Uncle, I think you'd better stay on the raft," said Axel.

Suddenly there was a deep rumble somewhere below, and Axel felt the raft vibrate under his feet. A fiery red line appeared all round them, and there was a fierce blast of heat too. Axel gulped, and realised they had jumped out of the frying pan and into the fire. Literally. Their raft was sitting at the bottom of one of those lava shafts his uncle had spoken of, on the solid rock cap.

Beneath them was a column of boiling-hot lava. They were deep inside a volcano, and it was going to erupt. So the rock cap beneath the raft was about to be blasted upwards. Axel gulped, and wondered what to do. Maybe they could get back out to the sea. But then there was another, much louder, rumble, and he knew they'd probably run out of time. Axel remembered what his uncle had said about this kind of shaft leading up to the surface. Maybe this was their only way out…

"Fascinating…" the professor murmured, completely ignoring Axel and climbing halfway into one of the openings. He was so intent on studying these new rocks that he had no idea of what was going on around him.

Axel scowled, and something inside him finally snapped. He strode across the raft, grabbed his uncle, and yanked him back out of the hole.

"Just listen to me for once, will you?" he muttered. "You have to stay on the raft because otherwise you'll probably get burned to a crisp, OK?"

"Er…why, yes, my boy," muttered the professor, surprised. "Although what's the problem? I really don't…" He caught sight of the fiery glow, and his eyes widened. "Hold on…" he said. "Are we in a…lava shaft?"

"Got it in one, Uncle," said Axel as the rumble grew and grew until it was a roar, and the floor of the shaft and the walls started vibrating so much his teeth ached. "And I think it's about to blow. Brace yourself!"

There was a huge BANG! and the raft flew up, riding the rocky floor as if it were some kind of flying carpet. It was certainly the only thing that stopped them being vapourised by the red-hot lava below it. They rose and rose and rose, the shaft walls crazily flashing past. Both of them screamed at the tops of their voices again, and shot out into daylight.

Axel parted company with the raft, tumbling head over heels through the air, glimpsing a vast crater below him, crashing at last into some soft soil and tumbling down a slope. He lay for a second, unable to believe he was alive. But eventually he raised his head and saw his uncle nearby.

The professor was sitting up, and had a rock in his hand.

"That was fun, wasn't it?" said the professor. "And so interesting too, even though we didn't make it all the way to the centre of the Earth. I can't wait to start planning another little trip. Where would you like to go next, Axel? How about a voyage beneath the sea? I know, we could build a rocket and fly to the moon. There must be some great rocks there…"

But Axel wasn't listening. He had his fingers stuck in his ears, and he was already trying to work out where they were and how to get home.

It was a tough job, of course…but someone had to do it!

THE RELUCTANT WARRIOR
THE STORY OF KING ALFRED AND THE BURNT LOAVES

LATE ONE COLD WINTER AFTERNOON in the Kingdom of Wessex, just as the sun was going down over the palace, Alfred closed the door of his chamber, leaned back against it, and sighed with contentment. He had done his duties for that day, and now he had some precious time to himself. Time to enjoy the thing he loved doing above all else in his life – reading.

Alfred was a prince in a royal family of Saxon warriors, tough men living in an age of iron and blood and fire. Wessex was threatened by the Vikings – wild, savage invaders from the cold lands of the north. Alfred had been trained to fight, and even though he was still very young, he had been in his share of bloody battles. But he hated war. In the last few years his father and three of his older brothers had been killed fighting the Vikings, leaving Alfred's last remaining brother, Ethelred, as king.

It all seemed so senseless, Alfred thought, looking through his narrow window.

The sky beyond it was swiftly turning black. Why couldn't men settle their differences without killing each other? Suddenly Alfred heard footsteps in the passage, then somebody pounded heavily on his door.

"Come in," yelled Alfred, and the door flew open to reveal a warrior, one of his brother's personal bodyguards. The man's face was grim.

"My lord, the Vikings have attacked again," he said. "The king is holding a war council in the great hall, and would like you to be there."

"I'm on my way," said Alfred, grabbing his sword and hurrying out.

He found the great hall crowded and bustling with activity. Ethelred was at the centre of everything, listening to reports and giving orders.

"It looks like we're outnumbered by a long way, little brother," he said, turning to Alfred. "Guthrum means to take our kingdom this time."

At first the Vikings had been sea-wolves, raiding settlements on the coast, and only in the summer months. They appeared out of the morning mist in their lean ships and killed anyone who stood up to them. Then they stole whatever they fancied, took the women and children as their slaves, left empty villages burning and were back in their northern homes before the freezing winds of winter turned the tips of the waves to ice.

But now they had a new warleader, a cruel, terrifying warrior called Guthrum, and he had his eyes on a much bigger prize. He had gathered a huge army of Vikings and kept it in Britain through three winters. He had defeated the other main English kingdoms – East Anglia, Northumbria and Mercia – and ruled them with an iron hand. He seemed to love looting monasteries and burning books, and Alfred really hated him for that.

Wessex alone stood proud and undefeated, like a stag surrounded by baying wolves, thought Alfred. But the wolves were growing stronger…

"So tell me something I don't know," he said, shrugging. "We'll just have to make sure that swine Guthrum doesn't get what he wants."

"Too right!" laughed Ethelred, and the brothers grinned at each other.

Ethelred was the second youngest, only a couple of years older than Alfred, and the two of them had always been particularly close. "He'll rue the day when he decided to tangle with us Wessex boys, won't he?"

The next morning, Ethelred's army met Guthrum's Vikings in a valley. Ethelred gave the order to halt, and the front rank of his warriors formed a shield wall – each man held his shield so it overlapped with that of the man next to him. Ethelred stood with his bodyguards, Alfred by his side.

Alfred gripped tight the hilt of his sword, and shifted his shield on his shoulder. One of the bodyguards was holding the battle standard, the great banner of Wessex. Alfred could see it streaming above him in the wind, a white dragon on a green background, the shiny silk snapping and flapping, the colours sharp and clear beneath the cold, iron-grey sky.

But he was more interested in Guthrum's warriors. Of course, Alfred had seen Vikings before, and they were always a fearsome sight, more like demons from hell than men. But these Vikings seemed especially huge and menacing, their faces battle-scarred and screwed up in hate.

They had their own shield wall, and a little further back, on the rising slope of the valley, stood a tall Viking surrounded by warriors. They were obviously his bodyguards, and Alfred realised he was looking at Guthrum himself. The Viking leader was dressed in black armour and a billowing black cloak, but he wore no helmet, and his corn-yellow hair blew free in the wind. Beside him an enormous warrior held the Viking standard, a great silken banner with a black Raven of Death on a blood-red square…

Soon the sky was filled with the thrum of arrows and the screams of men, the sound of pounding feet and the clashing of shield walls. The Vikings charged three times, but Ethelred's men held their ground, and the bloody work went on till the setting sun turned the whole world red, not just the trampled grass where the bodies lay. At last the armies pulled apart. Neither side was defeated, but each was too exhausted to fight on.

Alfred took off his helmet and wiped his forehead, grateful he was still alive. He had become separated from Ethelred in the fighting. Then one of his brother's bodyguards came running up. "My lord," said the man, whose face was splashed with blood. "The king is wounded…"

Alfred ran to his brother, but Ethelred was already dead when he got to him, an arrow deep in his throat. Alfred sank to his knees and wept.

"The king is dead," yelled a warrior. "Long live…King Alfred!"

Alfred rose to his feet and stood surrounded by cheering men, their sword blades flashing in the last rays of the setting sun. He felt sick and bewildered. He had never wanted to be king, and he had no idea how to do the job. But it looked like there was no getting out of it…

That winter and spring Alfred learned some hard lessons about war and being king. Guthrum's army struck again and again, and it seemed hardly a day went by when Alfred wasn't fighting battles with the Vikings. He rarely got a moment to himself, and barely had the time to open a book.

But things gradually began to improve. Wessex didn't fall to Guthrum, and Alfred knew he had inflicted heavy losses on his enemy. Alfred sat in his palace one evening, too tired to read, wondering what to do next. He was determined to end the fighting one way or another. Perhaps Guthrum might be willing to talk now… It had to be worth a try, thought Alfred.

So in the late summer, Alfred called a truce and asked Guthrum to meet him on the border. Alfred waited with his bodyguards, and Guthrum eventually arrived with his men. Alfred walked forward alone, Guthrum did the same and the two of them stood, face to face in the shifting, dappled sunlight beneath the branches of an ancient oak tree.

"So then, little Saxon princeling," said Guthrum, his cold, sea-green eyes fixed on Alfred's. "Have you come to kneel before me as your lord and master? I can be as kind and bountiful in peace as I am cruel in war."

"That's not what I've heard, Viking," said Alfred. "And I'm not here to surrender. I want to find a way for us to live in peace. Too many of my people have died fighting you. Although, if we keep killing your warriors at the same rate as lately, soon you won't have an army to invade with."

"Umm, you might have a point," murmured Guthrum, rubbing his chin and giving Alfred a crafty look. "You're certainly a tougher opponent than your father and brothers. Well then, how much will you offer me?"

Alfred frowned. He had heard that sometimes people could bribe the Vikings to leave them alone. Could it really be that easy? He supposed it could. It might take a lot of gold to do it – Guthrum was greedy, even for a Viking – but no amount of gold was worth more Saxon lives, was it?

"How much do you want?" said Alfred. "Maybe we can make a deal."

Guthrum smiled at him, his sharp, white teeth gleaming like a wolf's.

They settled on a figure at last, and then Alfred set about raising the money. He finally handed it all over to Guthrum just before Christmas.

It was a better Christmas than Alfred had been expecting, but he still felt very tired and sad. It seemed as if the palace was full of ghosts, the spirits of his father and brothers… His mother was long since dead too, so he knew what it was to be lonely, which is why he disbanded his army and sent his warriors home to celebrate the season with their families.

His bodyguards stayed in the palace because their lives were dedicated to protecting the king. But they didn't have much to do. Alfred drank a toast to peace, and passed some time at the Christmas feast. But he spent every other moment doing what he enjoyed most – reading, of course.

Alfred went to bed late on Twelfth Night. He fell asleep and dreamed of his parents and brothers. Then his dream turned into a nightmare of Vikings and battles, and Guthrum striding towards him over the bodies of Saxon warriors, Guthrum laughing, Guthrum roaring out his war cry…

Alfred woke with a start and leaped from his bed, the war cry still echoing in his mind. Or was it only there? Surely the sound was real! To his horror he heard the clang of swords and the screams of men. He went over to his window, saw dark shapes running in the courtyard, and a familiar figure with corn-yellow hair. Guthrum and his Vikings, in the palace! It was a sneak attack, just when Alfred was least expecting it.

Alfred's door flew open and one of his bodyguards ran in. "My lord," said the man. "Guthrum has broken the truce... We can't hold them back!"

Alfred grabbed his sword and ran to the great hall, where more of his bodyguards waited. But there was nothing they could do. Alfred's men were outnumbered. The palace was surrounded, and the Vikings were crashing their fists and sword hilts on the doors of the great hall itself.

"They're searching for you, my lord," said one of the bodyguards. "We must get you away before it's too late. There's not a moment to lose!"

Afterwards Alfred could remember little of what happened – the dash through darkened rooms, the secret door at the rear of the palace that made their escape possible. But he did look back as his bodyguards hurried him towards the forest. He saw Guthrum standing on the battlements, his sword raised in triumph, flames leaping behind him...

The next few weeks were difficult. Guthrum made it known there would be a rich reward for the man who brought him the Saxon king's head, and the Vikings hunted Alfred like a wolfpack with the scent of blood in its nostrils. Alfred and his men could move only at night, and made for the only place where they might find refuge – Athelney, the ancient heart of Wessex, an island in the middle of dense marshes.

Few people knew the secret paths to Athelney, and even fewer lived there. Alfred arrived on a rainy winter afternoon with a handful of his bodyguards. The rest hid in the countryside nearby to keep watch. Alfred looked at all that was left to him of his kingdom – a few shabby, low huts on a patch of muddy ground bordered by reeds and evil-smelling pools.

Suddenly he felt deeply tired, and had a great desire to get out of the rain. He went over to the nearest hut and knocked on the doorpost. An old lady emerged and glowered at him. "Yes?" she snapped. "What do you want? Can't you see I'm far too busy to be bothered by some silly boy?"

"Curb your tongue, old woman," growled one of Alfred's men, angrily moving towards her, hand on his hilt. "Don't you know this is your…"

"I think it might be better for the lady not to know who I am," said Alfred, holding

the warrior back. "I wondered if I might come inside," he added. "Your hut looks dry and warm. I promise you won't be harmed."

"Well…all right then," said the old woman, her eyes still narrowed with suspicion. "You can come in…but he can't," she added, pointing at the warrior who had spoken to her. "And none of the others can, neither."

The hut smelled of sweet herbs and good cooking, and there was a bright fire of logs in the hearth. Alfred warmed his hands while the old woman went back to what she had been doing, kneading dough into loaves. She was more friendly now, and chattered away as she worked.

Alfred was lost in his own thoughts and barely listened. At last the old woman put the loaves into the warm ashes round the edge of the fire to bake, then took a bunch of herbs from the wall and made for the door.

"Keep an eye on that bread for me, will you, dearie?" she said. "I'm just popping next door with these for my friend. I won't be long…bye!"

"What? Oh yes, of course…" said Alfred, but she was already gone.

He sighed and stared into the flames, and wondered for the thousandth time what he should do now. He felt a complete fool. Guthrum's trick had worked, and it seemed that the Vikings had won. The Saxon army was scattered, their king a fugitive hunted throughout the land that had been ruled by his family for generations. Maybe he should just give up.

Perhaps he could join a monastery. At least there he might be able to read. He reached beneath his damp cloak and pulled out a small book, the only one he had been able to bring with him from the palace. It was a book of old poems – tales of heroes fighting monsters, the last stands of warriors against overwhelming odds and sad stories of loss and longing.

Alfred sat reading, deeply engrossed, and didn't notice the smell of burning bread that gradually began to fill the hut. But the old woman did.

"Oh no!" she cried as she came in. She dashed over to the hearth and pulled the blackened loaves out of the ashes. But it was too late. "They're ruined," she moaned. "What have you been doing, you stupid, dozy boy?"

"I'm…I'm sorry. I really am," Alfred stammered. "I was reading my book, and I suppose I, er…got carried away and forgot about them…"

"Reading a book!" said the old lady, throwing the loaves at him. "So I'll have to go hungry tonight because you've been having fun. Well, thanks a lot! Maybe someday you'll learn to concentrate on what's important in life and not let people down. Now scram, before I really lose my temper!"

Alfred edged round her and hurried out of the hut. He walked to the edge of a pool and stood there in the drifting rain, feeling terribly guilty.

But the old woman's words had made him think. She was right in more ways than one. He should concentrate on what was important – and for the King of Wessex that meant beating Guthrum and making sure that the people of Wessex weren't at the mercy of a cruel and terrifying ruler. And if he did that, there would be plenty of time to read in the future…

Suddenly Alfred felt determined to fight, for his father and brothers and for all those who had died in the struggle with the Vikings. He took a deep breath, tucked the book inside his cloak and went to gather his men.

"Guthrum is definitely going to be sorry he tangled with us Wessex boys," he said. He felt as if the spirits of his dead father and brothers were there as well, Ethelred marching beside him, matching his stride…

Guthrum *was* sorry too. Over the next few months, Alfred planned and prepared. He sent secret messengers summoning his army to meet him in the spring. Then he went on the attack, ruthlessly harrying the enemy wherever they were. Eventually he faced Guthrum again in battle.

This time Alfred thrashed the Vikings, and trampled their banner beneath his feet. Guthrum kneeled, and the Saxons roared Alfred's name.

There were more Viking leaders, of course, and many more battles to come. But Wessex was the rock that broke the storm, and Alfred worked hard to keep his kingdom strong. He built fortresses, and created a navy to fight the Vikings at sea. But he also built monasteries and stocked their libraries with books, and sometimes he even found time to read them.

As for the old lady in Athelney…well, Alfred had a big abbey built there, so that he would always remember his darkest moment. And some say he made the old lady the abbess, while others say he just made her the chief cook. But whatever he did, she never, ever went hungry again.

And pretty soon the people of Wessex had given their king a new title. They named him King Alfred the Great. And we still call him that today!

THE GREAT MAN-MOUNTAIN

THE STORY OF GULLIVER IN LILLIPUT

GULLIVER WAS A MAN WHO LIKED TO TRAVEL. It wasn't just that he enjoyed visiting distant, exotic places. What he loved most was meeting new people, and learning as much as he could about them. So he went on many voyages, and saw many strange and wonderful things. And this is the story of his visit to the strangest, most incredible country of all.

The voyage started well enough. Gulliver and his fellow explorers headed for the South Seas, stopping to study plants or people wherever the fancy took them. Then one night their vessel ran into a storm and began to sink, and they had to abandon ship. But most of the crew were swept overboard while they were still trying to launch the lifeboat.

Soon Gulliver found himself alone in the sea, desperately struggling to keep his head above the water, until finally darkness swept over him…

He was woken by the warm sun on his face, and the lazy sound of surf hissing over a reef. He had survived! He realised the sea had dumped him on a beach –

and that he couldn't stand up. When he looked down, he saw he had been tied down while he slept. In fact, he was trussed up like a joint for roasting. Dozens of fine strings attached to tiny pegs in the sand criss-crossed his whole body.

Gulliver raised his head…and to his astonishment, he saw a tiny person standing on his chest looking back at him. The little man was no taller than a toy soldier, and was holding a miniature bow and arrow in his tiny hands. Gulliver felt a tickle of movement on his legs and body and, before long, the little archer was joined by a dozen more like him.

"I must be going mad…" Gulliver murmured at last. Then he yelled, "Get off me!" and the little archers screamed and ran for their lives.

Gulliver strained against his bonds and managed to free his arms. He instantly heard a soft whooshing noise and realised that the little archers were shooting at him. Their tiny arrows prickled into his hands and face like a host of wasp stings, several only just missing his eyes. The pain told him he wasn't mad, and that what was happening was all too real.

He saw now that there were hundreds of tiny people on the beach. The little archers were firing steadily at him, but the rest were fleeing in panic, screaming at the tops of their tiny voices. Suddenly Gulliver understood. To them he was a giant, so it was hardly surprising they thought he might be a threat. How could they know he wouldn't hurt anyone, big or small?

It also occurred to Gulliver that this was a fantastic opportunity for him to learn. He had never encountered anything like these little people, and he had so much to ask them. Then a tiny arrow landed right on the end of his nose, and he realised he would have to make friends with them first. It might take a while, but that was fine. He prided himself on being patient.

"OK, you win!" he said, smiling. "I promise I won't hurt you." Then he put his arms down – making quite sure there were no tiny people under them to be crushed – and lay still. "Oh yes, I er… surrender," he added.

To Gulliver's great relief, the little archers stopped shooting, and the others overcame their fear and started to return. Within a few minutes, the beach was full of activity, all the tiny people hustling and bustling…

They built a big trolley, winched Gulliver onto it, then harnessed dozens of tiny horses to one end. Soon he was being carried through a countryside of tiny hills and streams, tiny trees and hedges, and tiny fields with tiny cattle and sheep in them. There were even tiny villages full of tiny people who came out to gawp. Gulliver gawped back, enthralled.

At last the trolley creaked to a halt, and there before Gulliver was an amazing sight – a perfect little city surrounded by a wall, the battlements full of tiny people yelling with excitement. Gulliver was winched off the trolley and his bonds were removed – although not before one of his ankles was chained to a large rock some distance from the city's gates. He gave the chain a tug, and found that he couldn't break it.

After a while, a column of tiny horsemen cantered out, all of them wearing shiny breastplates and helmets with nodding plumes. They formed two ranks facing each other, raised tiny trumpets and blew a fanfare. Then a tiny coach drawn by four tiny white horses emerged from the gateway, swept between the ranks of horsemen, and came to a halt. Two tiny footmen ran up to open the door, and a tiny man climbed out.

He was wearing a tiny golden crown, lavish clothes and fancy shoes with rather high heels. Gulliver immediately guessed this was someone important, although he couldn't help noticing the little man was very small, even for an inhabitant of this country of tiny people. He had a little round tummy, short skinny legs and a snooty expression on his face.

The crowd on the battlements cheered and clapped, and the little man waved vaguely in their direction. Then he turned to Gulliver, and spoke.

"I trust you are ready to humbly beg my forgiveness for your arrival on the shores of my empire," he said. "I don't remember giving permission for anyone like you to visit us. In fact, who – or rather, what – are you?"

"My name is Gulliver, and I suppose I'm, er…a human being," our hero replied. "My ship went down in a storm and I was washed up on your beach. I really am terribly sorry if I've caused you any trouble…"

"A human being?" scoffed the little man. "That's utterly ridiculous. We are proper-sized human beings, while you are obviously a giant. And as for your name – well, I couldn't possibly say anything so barbarous. I shall call you the Great Man-Mountain." The crowd burst into cheering and applause again, and the little man gave them another vague wave.

"Right, er…that's fine," said Gulliver, trying to be friendly. "And would you mind telling me who you are?"

"Me? I am the Emperor of Lilliput, of course," the little man spluttered crossly, "Lord of All I Survey, High and Mighty Ruler, Conqueror of…"

"Ah, so your country is called Lilliput," said Gulliver, leaning forward eagerly. "How fascinating! There's just so much I want to ask you!"

"Really?" said the emperor, looking rather puzzled. "What about?"

"Oh, the kind of food you eat, the houses you live in," said Gulliver. "Your history, your gods… I want to know absolutely everything."

"I'm afraid that all sounds very boring," said the emperor, and there was a murmur of agreement from the crowd. "In any case, I haven't got time to answer a lot of stupid questions, and I doubt anyone else has either. This audience is over. I'll decide what to do with you later."

"Please, hang on a minute, er…Your Majesty," said Gulliver, slightly irritated by the casual way in which this tiny man was dismissing him. But he told himself to relax and stay calm. He would have to try harder…and keep his patience. "I'm not a boring person, er… I mean giant," he said, smiling. "Honestly, I can be lots of fun when you get to know me."

"Is that so?" said the emperor. "I have to say it's been awfully dull around here recently… A spot of fun would be good. Well, don't just sit there, Man-Mountain. Show me what you can do. And make it jolly."

Gulliver decided that perhaps he ought to behave like a giant, seeing as that's the way the Lilliputians thought of him… So he quickly picked up one of the emperor's tiny footmen and gently deposited him in the palm of his other hand. The little man lay there looking scared out of his wits.

Gulliver smiled and held him up to the watching crowd on the wall.

"Shall I eat him?" he said.

Some of the tiny people screamed "No!" But quite a few screamed "Yes!"

Gulliver laughed and shook his head. "I was only joking!" he said. Then he lowered his hand onto the city wall, and simply allowed the footman to scramble off. The tiny man was laughing himself now, mostly with relief, but with some pleasure too.

"Right," said Gulliver, leaving his hand where it was. "Anyone want a thrilling ride down to the ground?" Many of the tiny people backed off, but plenty eagerly stepped forward, and Gulliver allowed three to climb onto his palm. Then he swung them in a high, graceful arc through the air, and over to where the emperor was standing. They jumped off, screaming with excitement and pleasure and calling out to their friends.

"Well, I'm impressed, Man-Mountain," said the emperor, smiling up at him. "I am therefore happy to grant you leave to stay in my empire for the time being, and to be in my service. Now I should like a ride myself."

"Why, of course, Your Majesty," said Gulliver. "Climb aboard…"

And so began a strange time for Gulliver. The Great Man-Mountain provided the emperor and people of Lilliput with lots of entertainment. He gave thrilling rides to hundreds of Lilliputians. He sat still while he let hundreds more clamber over him, examining his clothes and face and hair, and generally using him as some kind of adventure playground. It was rather undignified, but Gulliver thought it was all in a good cause.

After a while, he tried asking the tiny people questions, but they were always too busy enjoying themselves to give him any proper answers. So he asked the emperor if he could speak to some Lilliputian historians. But to Gulliver's huge frustration, the emperor simply waved the idea away. The emperor did insist that several hours were set aside each day for his own exclusive access to The Great Man-Mountain, though.

He liked Gulliver to put him in the top pocket of his jacket, and to stand up so that he could survey his empire from a great height. Gulliver enjoyed it too. It was fun to look down on the city with its narrow streets and little buildings and crowds of tiny people, although Gulliver often found himself gazing into the distance, longing to do some exploring.

"Er…I was wondering if I could ask a favour, Your Majesty," he said one day.

The emperor was in his top pocket, peering through a telescope. "A favour?" he answered. "Ask away, Man-Mountain. Feel free."

"That's just it, Your Majesty," said Gulliver. "I don't feel free at all, and I'd like to. Is there any chance you could have me…unchained?"

"Oh no, definitely not," said the emperor, scowling. "I can't have you blundering about causing havoc with those giant feet of yours! Besides, I want you here, ready to entertain me whenever I desire it. Considering what it's costing me to keep you fed, it really is the least you can do."

Gulliver scowled now too. Three times a day, at breakfast, lunch and dinner, a procession of little wagons brought him food and drink. Some carried tiny barrels of water or ale. Others were heaped with cooked meat of various kinds, tiny sides of beef and pork, and tiny whole lambs and chickens. Still others contained piles of teeny-tiny vegetables and fruit.

Gulliver always ate everything, and at first he had felt guilty. The emperor had told him he got through the same amount in a day as the average Lilliputian family consumed in ten years. But the emperor had said it so many times, Gulliver's guilt had at last turned into irritation. He couldn't help having a big appetite, could he? After all, he was a giant!

"Well then, Your Majesty," Gulliver said grumpily, "have you seen enough for today? Or are there any other services I can perform for you?"

"Not that I can think of at the moment," said the emperor. "But I…"

"Good," said Gulliver, plucking the emperor from his pocket and returning him to the ground. "See you tomorrow…worse luck," he muttered under his breath. Then he sat down with his back to the emperor and the city.

He brooded for ages, hardly even feeling the crowd of Lilliputians swarming all over him, although he did absent-mindedly stop one tiny boy from climbing into his nostril. Gulliver wondered what he had to do to get some answers to his questions. He had been in Lilliput for several weeks now, and he knew no more about it than on the day he had arrived. He didn't even know if there had been any other survivors from his ship, or how he would eventually get home. Not that he wanted to leave yet. He was determined to learn something, although the Lilliputians seemed equally determined not to take any of his questions seriously. Gulliver sighed deeply, and resolved to stay patient a little while longer.

The next day, the emperor arrived as usual for his time with the Great Man-Mountain. Gulliver had already decided to be especially nice to him, to make up for his grumpiness of the day before. But just as he was about to put the emperor in his pocket, a tiny horseman came cantering up.

"Your Majesty, I bring evil tidings!" the messenger said, his voice trembling. "The King of Blefuscu has declared war on us. He's gathered a great invasion fleet, and it looks like he means to attack us…today!"

The emperor went pale and shouted at his officials, who ran around in total panic. Gulliver assumed that Blefuscu was a neighbouring country – and he realised that this might be his chance to get what he wanted…

"Excuse me, Your Majesty," he said. "Could I make a suggestion?"

"Not now, Man-Mountain," groaned the emperor. He put his hand to his brow and struck a tragic pose. "Can't you see? I'm having a crisis!"

"Yes, I know," said Gulliver. "And I think I might be able to help."

"You?" said the emperor, looking confused. "But…but how?"

"I gather these Blefuscans are the same size as you Lilliputians," said Gulliver. The emperor shrugged, and nodded. "Well then, don't you think that a…Great Man-Mountain could very easily sort them out for you?"

"Why, of course…" said the emperor. He began to smile. "You may have your uses after all, Man-Mountain. Unchain the giant, you men!"

"Wait a second," said Gulliver. "I'll only help on two conditions: you have to promise not to keep me chained up when I return, and to answer all my questions. Is it a deal?"

"Yes, yes, whatever…" muttered the emperor, frowning and vaguely waving his hand. "Just get on with it, will you? And don't take all day!"

"OK, keep your hair on," muttered Gulliver. "Where do I have to go?"

The emperor and his subjects all pointed in a particular direction, and Gulliver set off, their cheering ringing in his ears. He strode across the land, being careful not to tread on any houses or people, and soon came to a sandy beach. And there, on the other side of a narrow channel, was Blefuscu. Gulliver took off his jacket and shoes and waded into the sea.

Gulliver arrived to find a host of tiny ships in a little harbour. He took hold of all their anchor chains, tying them together and pulling the whole lot out behind him. Of course, the Blefuscans were terrified, and most of them screamed and leaped into the sea. But some fought back, and Gulliver felt the familiar, painful prickling of tiny arrows in his hands and arms.

The sea was cold, the current strong, and in the middle of the channel it even pulled Gulliver off his feet. He struggled for a while, and glimpsed an island in the distance, beyond Blefuscu…then his feet touched sand again, and he turned towards Lilliput. He left the Blefuscan ships bobbing offshore and crawled up the beach, relieved to be on dry land at last.

"Well done, Man-Mountain!" said a voice. Gulliver looked up and saw the emperor standing nearby. Behind him a crowd of tiny people was buzzing with excitement. "Now I want you to bring those ships in a little closer so we can start getting my army aboard. We'll soon show those Blefuscans a thing or two, especially with you leading the invasion…"

"Oh no, I'm not doing that," Gulliver replied. "What do you think I am? I might be a giant to you, but I'm not an ogre. Besides, we've got a deal. I stop the invasion, and you answer all my questions – remember?"

"Who cares about your stupid questions?" hissed the emperor. "You are my servant, Man-Mountain, and you will obey my orders instantly…"

"Right, that's it," said Gulliver, his patience snapping. "I can see I'm not going to find out anything while I'm here, and frankly I don't really care any more. I'd like to say I've enjoyed my stay in your country, Your Majesty, but I haven't, not one little bit. And now I'm off. Cheerio!"

Gulliver waded into the water and gathered the fleet's anchor chains once more. Meanwhile, the crowd was booing, and the emperor was hopping with anger. "Stop!" he squeaked. "I utterly forbid you to leave!"

Gulliver took no notice. He headed out to sea, and towards the island he had glimpsed beyond Blefuscu, pulling the Blefuscan ships behind him. Anywhere would be better than Lilliput, he thought, even if it was a desert island. Although, as he discovered, he couldn't have chosen a better place. For when he arrived he found the lifeboat from his ship washed up on the beach…

Soon Gulliver was sailing for home, with enough food and tiny barrels of ale and water from the Blefuscan fleet's supplies to keep him going for days. He gripped the tiller as a breeze filled the lifeboat's single sail, a little fed up that his stay in Lilliput seemed to have been such a waste of time. Then he smiled, realising that he had learned several things after all.

Gulliver knew now that people of any size could be unpleasant and vain – and also that he might not be quite as patient as he had always thought. Mind you, he couldn't wait to start planning a new voyage…

But that, of course, would be another story.

SHADOW OF FEAR

THE STORY OF ALEXANDER THE GREAT AND HIS HORSE, BUCEPHALUS

IT ISN'T EASY BEING A ROYAL PRINCE, as young Alexander had long since discovered. He was the son of King Philip and Queen Olympias of Macedon, the country that lies to the north of Greece. But Alexander's parents were rather difficult people, and they hadn't got on with each other for years.

Queen Olympias loved her son, and he loved his mother, of course. Yet Alexander realised that to most people she was, well…quite strange and scary. There were even whispers that she was a witch. She did seem to know a lot of spells and recipes for potions, and she always had a couple of deadly poisonous snakes wrapped round her, even in bed.

Philip was a stern ruler and a mighty warrior, and was often away fighting. So there were times when Alexander barely saw him. Philip liked to keep his son busy, though, and made sure he had plenty of tutors – grizzled warriors to teach him how to fight with sword and spear, and wise counsellors to help him learn the dark arts of being a king. While other boys of his age enjoyed themselves, Alexander trained or studied.

Not that he really minded. He worked hard, hoping to impress his father. Besides, he was very ambitious. He longed to be a mighty warrior when he grew up, just like Philip, and a worthy heir to him as well.

One day, Alexander was in the palace courtyard, practising his sword-fighting skills with a tutor, when suddenly he heard the clatter of hooves and the chinking of weapons and armour. He turned and saw his father gallop in through the gateway on his great black warhorse. As ever, a special band of mounted warriors – The Companions – followed him.

"Father, you're home at last!" Alexander cried out, and ran over to him. It was late afternoon. The low sun was behind Philip and his long shadow stretched right across the courtyard's flagstones. Alexander smiled up at him, at that almost forgotten face with its jagged scar, the ugly evidence of an eye lost in battle years ago. Philip didn't smile back at his son.

"So, Alexander…" he said, his voice deep and powerful. "I seem to have interrupted your sword practice. We can't have that, can we, lads?"

There was a murmur of agreement from The Companions. They had fanned out behind Philip, and Alexander found himself being stared at by this band of seriously hard men sitting easily on their big, strong horses.

"We didn't ask the young master to stop, though, did we, my lord?" said one of the warriors, and they all grinned. Alexander felt his cheeks flush.

"No, quite right," said Philip. "Carry on, then, Alexander. Come to think of it, I've never seen you using a proper sword before, only a toy one. So this is an excellent opportunity for you to show me what you can do."

Alexander went through all the exercises he usually did with his tutor, a wiry old warrior – thrusting and parrying, dodging and feinting, fighting with a shield and without one. He concentrated as hard as he could, ignoring the ache in his muscles and the sweat dripping off his face. He deliberately didn't look at his father, but he was constantly aware of him.

"Stop, I've seen enough!" Philip growled at last. Alexander met his father's one-eyed gaze and waited for the verdict. "Not bad…" said Philip, and Alexander smiled. Philip hadn't finished, though. "But not wonderful, either. And I was better when I was your age. A lot better."

Then he dug his heels in his horse's flanks and cantered off across the courtyard without so much as a backward glance, his men clattering along after him. Alexander watched them go, his smile now a grimace, the sweat cooling on his skin. A cloud passed over the sun, and he shivered…

Alexander swallowed his disappointment that time. Philip came to see him train every day, and Alexander tried even harder to impress him. But his nerves made him clumsy, and Philip was quick to tell him so. It was exactly the same with his studies. With Philip there, Alexander's mind stubbornly stayed empty, and he stammered and made stupid mistakes.

Philip would scowl, and tut-tut, and shake his head, then go off hunting with The Companions, refusing to take Alexander with him. And after a while Alexander could barely bring himself to look his father in the face.

There was another problem too. One evening Philip held a great feast, and Alexander listened as The Companions drank their wine and told loud stories about the king's courage and his victories and conquests. The warrior sitting next to Alexander turned and glanced at him curiously.

"Hey, why so glum and tight-lipped, young master?" he said. "Your father is a great man, and he will leave you a magnificent kingdom."

Alexander didn't reply. That was just it – there would be nothing left for him to achieve. How could he hope to match his father's success, let alone surpass it? Alexander was beginning to fear he would never be as good as his father at anything, never live up to his expectations, always be in his great shadow. So perhaps there was no point in even trying...

The next day, Alexander didn't train or study. He passed the morning and afternoon with his mother and her maids, listening to their chatter and playing with the snakes. In the early evening, just before supper, he heard heavy footsteps thudding down the corridor. Suddenly the doors to his mother's chamber were rudely thrust open. Philip stood there scowling.

"I think you owe me an explanation, Alexander," he growled. "Why aren't you with your tutors? They tell me they haven't seen you all day."

"I don't know…" murmured Alexander, gently stroking the head of a snake and not looking at his father. "I just didn't feel like it, I suppose."

"Well, that's not good enough," said Philip, his face dark with anger.

"Oh, leave him alone, you big bully," said Olympias, and her maids tittered. "He's happier here with us girls, aren't you, my little viper?"

Alexander didn't say anything. He glanced at his father, waiting for him to start shouting and yelling at him and the queen, and maybe even drag him out of the chamber. Philip, however, did none of those things. He stared at Alexander for an instant…then turned on his heel and left.

Alexander smiled, pleased with this small victory over his father after weeks of worry and pressure. Then his smile faded. It was one thing to get back at Philip by pretending to prefer being with his mother and her maids, but deep down, Alexander knew he could never be truly happy unless he became a mighty warrior and a worthy heir to his father. Now he felt he might just have cut himself off from any chance of doing that.

The next morning, he half hoped his father would lose his temper and simply order him to start training and studying again. But Philip didn't, and coolly ignored him instead. The same happened the next day, and the next, and the day after that… and Alexander began to feel very unhappy.

He soon got bored with sitting in his chamber brooding, or mooching round the palace avoiding his tutors. One morning, he found himself down by the royal stables. He had always loved animals, so he hung round for a while, helping the stable boys do their work. Somehow it seemed to make his unhappiness easier to bear, and he got into the habit of going to the stables every day. He learned a great deal about horses, and soon became a skilled rider.

Alexander would watch his father ride out with The Companions, off for a day's hunting, wishing he could go too. If only he could explain to his father how he felt, tell him how badly he wanted to discover what he had to do to impress him! But Alexander didn't know where to start, and he knew his father would never give him any help. It wasn't Philip's way.

And that's the way things might have carried on – if it hadn't been for a visit to the palace by a horse trader from Thessaly, the country to the south of Macedon. The man's name was Philoneicus, and he came once a year with fine horses to sell. He would line them up on the plain outside the palace walls, and Philip and The Companions would inspect them.

It was a warm spring morning, the sun just climbing above the eastern mountains. A crowd of locals and servants from the palace gathered to watch the trading,

Alexander following everyone else, and there was a feeling of carnival in the air. Philip was talking to Philoneicus, and The Companions were standing nearby, laughing at something that had been said. There was always plenty of rough banter on these occasions, and Alexander realised it was all part of the bargaining that went on.

"So, Philoneicus, what have you got for me?" said Philip with a smile. "Another bunch of worn-out nags? This lot don't look very promising."

"I am truly hurt that you should think I would bring you anything less than the very best, my lord," said Philoneicus. "Although everyone knows the mighty Philip has a keen eye when it comes to choosing horses…"

"Spare me the flattery," said Philip, laughing. "I've heard it all before. You had better not be wasting my time, Philoneicus. I'm a busy man."

"No, no, my lord," the trader said hastily. "I have first-class mounts for your men. And I also have something special, a steed fit for a great king!"

Alexander saw Philoneicus nod to one of his own men, who tugged on a rope and brought forward the horse it was attached to. Alexander caught his breath, his eyes widening in wonder. He had never seen a horse like it before – a tall, beautiful bay stallion, its long, elegant legs prancing, its glossy reddish-brown coat gleaming in the sunlight, its head held high and proud, a white flash in the shape of an ox-head on its long muzzle.

The crowd murmured its appreciation, and Philoneicus grinned.

"Umm, not bad, you old horsethief," said Philip. "I'll admit it's a good-looking beast. But it depends on the price you're asking… Not that I'm interested, you understand – especially as you always try to cheat me."

"I would only be cheating myself if I asked you for any less than…" Philoneicus paused, suddenly serious. "Thirteen silver talents, my lord."

Now the crowd gasped, and The Companions muttered. Alexander was stunned too. He knew that thirteen silver talents was an enormous amount of money. But Philip only raised his scarred eyebrow, and smiled faintly.

"That much, eh?" he said, looking as if he were bored. "Oh well," he sighed. "I suppose I'd better have a closer look at this marvel…"

A hush fell over the crowd, and all eyes were on Philip as he walked slowly forward. All eyes, that is, except those of Alexander, whose gaze was fixed on the horse. He could tell from the way it tossed its head and whinnied and strained at the rope that it was very nervous. It was also strong, and several times almost pulled over the man holding the rope.

Then something happened that nobody else spotted. The low sun was directly behind them, and the horse suddenly caught a glimpse of its own shadow moving across the dusty ground in front of it. Alexander could see the creature was spooked, but at almost the same moment a longer shadow fell across the horse's – that of Philip as he drew near.

The horse's reaction was instant. It reared up, kicking out with its iron-shod hooves, snorting and neighing in fear and distress. The man holding him nearly let slip the rope, and several of the trader's servants had to help him. A great struggle ensued, the powerful horse rearing, the men trying to hold on, and the crowd screaming and yelling with excitement.

Philip backed off and stood frowning while The Companions loudly called out advice to the horse trader's men, and made fun of them. All the noise made the poor horse even more frightened, and Alexander's heart ached to see this beautiful animal so tormented, its eyes rolling in terror.

Eventually the horse stopped rearing, and stood there pawing the ground instead, its flanks heaving, tremors quivering over its skin.

"My apologies, mighty king!" murmured Philoneicus, hurrying up to Philip. "My men are to blame, of course. One of them has obviously upset the horse somehow. It never, ever, behaves like this normally. Why, you couldn't hope to find a calmer, more even-tempered beast anywhere…"

"Don't talk rubbish, Philoneicus," snapped Philip. "I know a decent horse when I see one, and I'll grant you that animal has lots of potential. Maybe even thirteen silver talents' worth – if it was properly broken in, that is. But it obviously isn't. The beast is practically wild, and it's far too wilful. I'm an excellent horseman myself, and I don't think I could ride him. Come on, lads. I'm not in the mood for buying today anyway."

Philip turned to go, and Philoneicus scurried after him, pleading. "Ten talents, my lord," he said, but Philip shook his head. "Eight…seven…"

Suddenly Alexander realised this was the perfect opportunity to impress his father. Unlike the king, Alexander felt that he could ride the horse. It was just a question of making sure it didn't see its shadow… But Alexander also knew he would have to set the whole thing up properly, do it the way his father would. He had to be cool and controlled, like Philip was with Philoneicus, like the men bantering with each other.

Now he saw that was probably what Philip had been seeking from him all along – he wanted a son who would stand up to him and not give in…

So Alexander took a deep breath and stepped forward. "I'll buy the horse, Philoneicus," he said. "And I'll pay you thirteen talents for it too."

The crowd fell silent again, but the hush this time was different, full of anticipation and excitement. Everyone knew about the tension between the king and his son, of course. Philip stopped, and slowly turned round to face him. Alexander lifted his chin and stared right back at his father, almost as if he were laying down a challenge to him. Philip scowled.

"Don't be ridiculous, boy," said Philip. "You couldn't ride the beast – nobody could. And where are you going to get thirteen silver talents? It will take you a long time to save that much out of your pocket money."

The Companions laughed, and the crowd joined in. Alexander stood there surrounded by jeering, mocking adults, but he didn't take his eyes off his father's face, not for a second. And Philip didn't look away.

"I think you're wrong, Father," said Alexander. "So why don't we make it a wager?

I bet you I can ride that horse. If I do, you have to give me the money to buy it. If I don't succeed, well, I'll have to find the money to pay Philoneicus somehow. Although I'll probably be dead in any case."

There was no laughter now. "My lord, it would be far too dangerous for the young master…" murmured one of The Companions, the others all agreeing. Philoneicus joined in, obviously terrified of what would happen to him if Alexander were killed. Philip raised a hand to silence them.

"Well then, Father," said Alexander at last. "Do we have a bet or not?"

Philip looked at his son with his one eye for an instant…and nodded, a faint smile playing round his lips. Alexander briefly smiled back at him, then turned and headed towards the horse. The crowd was buzzing.

"Give me the rope," he said. The trader's men handed it over, and fled beyond the reach of the horse's hooves. Alexander felt the animal pull against him, but he gently forced the horse to turn so it was facing the sun, and unable to see its shadow. "Stay clear, everybody!" he called out.

Now he moved in close. He stroked the horse's neck, and whispered to it, using all the skills he had learned working in the stables, and soon he could feel the animal begin to calm down. "There, there," he murmured. "Everything will be all right, you'll see. You will be my horse and I will be your master, and together we will do the most marvellous things…"

And when he judged that the moment was right, Alexander gripped the horse's thick mane and swung himself onto its back. He dug his heels into its flanks, and the horse galloped away faster than the wind, its hooves drumming across the dusty ground. Alexander let it run for a while, then brought it round with a tug on its mane and returned to the palace walls.

He rode up to his father and brought the horse to a halt. Alexander looked down at Philip…and Philip grinned up at him. The Companions and the crowd were cheering, and Philoneicus was looking very relieved.

"Not bad, Alexander," murmured Philip, patting the horse's neck. "In fact, I have to say that I'm rather impressed. I do believe I did a great deal of riding when I was your age. Although the truth is that I was…"

"Yes, Father?" whispered Alexander, his mouth suddenly dry.

"Nowhere near as good as you are!" Philip said, and laughed. "And I would never have stood up to my father the way you've just stood up to me. I can see that you're going to need a much bigger kingdom than I can ever provide for you. I'm sure you'll get it too, and that's fine. It's just the way it should be." Then he turned to The Companions behind him. "Behold my son, who will be a far greater king than me!" he roared.

The Companions yelled their approval, and Alexander's heart swelled with pride. And later that day, father and son went hunting together…

Philip paid Philoneicus his thirteen talents, and Alexander named his horse Bucephalus, which is Greek for Ox-Head. Alexander succeeded Philip as King of Macedon, and Philip was right – in a few short years, Alexander conquered a huge swathe of countries, from Greece to the borders of faraway India. He rode his trusty horse, Bucephalus, in every battle, and long before he died people called him Alexander the Great.

And he always knew his father would have been proud of him.

THE SNAKE-HAIRED KILLER

THE STORY OF PERSEUS AND MEDUSA THE GORGON

PERSEUS WAS SITTING BEHIND A MYRTLE BUSH at the side of the small house where he lived with his mother, Danae, counting the minutes until her guest left. He always hid there when King Polydectes came to call. The king didn't like Perseus, and Perseus didn't much like Polydectes either. He was a nasty piece of work – a greedy, deeply cunning, violent man.

So it was very worrying that he wanted to marry Perseus's mother.

Perseus sighed. Things had always been tough for the pair of them. They were exiles from the Greek city of Tiryns, and had come to the island of Seriphos when Perseus was still a baby. Danae had never told Perseus why they'd been exiled, or who his father was, and there had certainly been no man around the house while he was growing up.

They were poor, and life on Seriphos had been hard enough – and now Polydectes, king of the island, had made it complicated too. Danae had told him she wasn't interested, but he wouldn't take no for an answer…

Suddenly Perseus heard footsteps, and he peeked between the leaves of the bush. At last Polydectes was leaving the house with his bodyguards, a bunch of men almost as ugly and evil as their lord. Perseus studied the king's face, expecting to see him looking sullen and bad-tempered, his usual expression after the lovely Danae had refused him once more. But Perseus was horrified to see that this time Polydectes was smiling.

Perseus waited until the king and his men had definitely gone, then he hurried into the house. His mother was ladling lamb stew into two bowls.

"Oh, there you are, Perseus," she said. "Your supper is ready."

"Never mind that, Mother," said Perseus. "Why was Polydectes looking so pleased with himself? You haven't said you'll marry him, have you?"

"Don't be silly," said Danae. "I told him I wouldn't be his wife, just as I always do. Mind you, he did try a different tack today – he asked me for a reason. And I couldn't admit I simply didn't like him, could I? That would have been rather rude. So I had to come up with something else."

"What did you say, then?" Perseus murmured, his heart sinking.

"Just that I couldn't possibly get married while I still had you to look after," said Danae, smiling at him innocently. "I meant until you were grown-up, of course. Have I done the wrong thing, Perseus?"

"Er…don't worry about it," said Perseus, not wanting to upset her, although now he was anxious himself. He thought she might have signed his death warrant. If King Polydectes believed he was the only obstacle between him and what he wanted, Perseus felt certain he was doomed. It could only be a question of time before the king's men came for him…

A few days later, a royal messenger brought him an invitation – to the king's birthday party! Danae wasn't invited, which seemed very strange. But Perseus felt he didn't dare turn the invitation down. Polydectes would probably take that as some kind of insult and have him killed anyway.

Perseus knew he had a problem as soon as he arrived at the palace gates. There was a long queue of young men waiting to go in, each of them dressed in fine clothes, each carrying a fabulous gift for the king. But Perseus's clothes were old and threadbare, and he had brought no gift. He and his mother simply couldn't afford to buy anything.

The others in the queue pointed at him and laughed, and Perseus felt his cheeks burning with shame. There was nothing he could do about being poor, though, except keep his head up and look everyone in the eye, which he did. He took his place at the back of the queue and waited.

"Right, lads, step this way!" a grinning palace guard cried out after a while, opening the gates and beckoning them in. "The king awaits you!"

Polydectes was sitting on his throne in the great hall, flanked by his bodyguards. The young men in the queue approached him, one by one, bowing low and handing over their gifts, until only Perseus was left. He kneeled before the king, conscious that everyone in the room was staring.

"Hi, Your Majesty!" he said. "And, er…happy birthday, too!"

"Why, thank you, Perseus," Polydectes said smoothly. "But is that all I'm getting from you, a mere greeting? Have you no gift for me? As you can see," he said, waving at the glittering heap of costly gifts beside him, "the other young men of Seriphos have been very generous. But then I suppose I shouldn't have expected much from a poor, landless exile."

The bodyguards guffawed, and the young men tittered. Perseus felt his cheeks grow hot again, although it was anger that made them burn this time. So that was what Polydectes was up to, he thought. The king had brought him here to be humiliated in front of the island's rich boys. Well, that wasn't going to happen. Perseus had as much pride as anybody.

"I'm sorry to be such a disappointment," he said calmly. "Is there anything in particular you want? Name it and I promise before everyone here that I'll do my best to get it for you. Other than my mother, that is."

Polydectes gave him a cold, nasty smile. Perseus thought he looked like a snake that was about to strike. "What a generous offer!"

the king said. "Actually, there is something I want…" His smile vanished, and his eyes glittered with malice. "The head of the Gorgon Medusa!" he hissed.

Perseus recoiled as if he *had* been bitten by a snake. It was a terrible thing to ask of him. Gorgons were hideous, scary, lethal creatures – just looking at the face of one could turn you into stone. And Medusa was the most terrifying Gorgon of them all. Many great heroes had tried to kill her, but none had succeeded. More importantly, none had survived…

Suddenly Perseus realised that Polydectes wasn't trying to humiliate him. This was a plot to get rid of him completely! Perseus had promised to do whatever Polydectes wanted, so he would have to agree. Unless he wanted to be mocked for the rest of his life, that is. And of course, with Perseus out of the way, Polydectes would force Danae to marry him.

"So be it," Perseus said firmly, his head held high, his eyes locked on those of Polydectes. Then he strode out of the hall, the sound of his footsteps on the marble floor echoing behind him. The king, the bodyguards and the young men laughed and jeered at him, but he took no notice. He kept right on walking until he had left the palace of Polydectes far behind him.

He stopped eventually, and sat on a rock by the roadside, in the shade of an ancient olive tree. Then he thought about what he had agreed to do, and he felt sick. How could he possibly kill one of the scariest monsters of all time? He had never done anything remotely like that in his life. He didn't even know where to find her. The whole idea was totally crazy.

Suddenly Perseus heard strange, haunting music, and saw that the air in front of him was shimmering. Soon it took on the shape of a tall, beautiful woman. She was wearing a warrior's helmet with a nodding horsehair plume, carrying a spear and shield, and was surrounded by a golden glow. Perseus knew immediately she was an Olympian immortal.

"Hail, mighty Goddess!" he said, falling to his knees, which seemed the correct thing to do. "Er...sorry to ask, but which one are you, exactly?"

"Why, I'm Athena of course, young man," she said, sounding miffed. Her booming voice seemed to fill Perseus's head. "I'm surprised you don't recognise me. There are plenty of statues in my temples, after all."

"I'm sorry, Your Marvellousness..." said Perseus. "Please forgive me."

"Of course," said Athena, smiling at him now. "Well, I won't beat about the bush, Perseus – we immortals are very busy, you know, always sorting out the messes you humans get yourselves into. And that's why I'm here. I've come to give you some help in finding Medusa...and defeating her."

"Great!" said Perseus. He jumped up and almost gave her a hug, but thought better of it. Then he scowled, suddenly suspicious. "Don't take this the wrong way," he said. "I'm very grateful for any help I can get. But why are you doing this? The gods don't care about me, do they?"

"Well, one of us does," said Athena, "and he's very important too. Tell me, Perseus, did your lovely mother ever mention a brief encounter with Almighty Zeus, Lord of the Gods...some time before you were born?"

"Are you saying...what I think you're saying?" murmured Perseus, hardly able to grasp the thought that had just popped into his mind.

"My lips are sealed," Athena replied. "Telling tales of that kind can get you into a lot of trouble. For instance, your grandfather didn't believe your mother when she said your father was a, er...certain well-known god. He thought she was lying, which is why he exiled the pair of you."

"And I suppose she didn't tell me about it herself because she didn't think I would believe her either," said Perseus.

Athena just shrugged.

"I wouldn't have," Perseus muttered. "I mean, it's all very well having a god for a father, but he hasn't done much for me so far, has he?"

"Now, now, young man," Athena said sternly. "You have to remember that running the universe is a full-time job. And Zeus has asked me to say that he's sorry he's never paid you a visit, but that he'll always make sure you get help when you need it. Which brings us to your problem."

"Fair enough," Perseus said, shrugging. There was no point in arguing. Zeus might not be an ideal father, but he could prove to be very useful in the current situation. "So what's the plan?" Perseus continued. "Wait, I know – Zeus zaps Medusa with a thunderbolt or two, then you swoop down and chop off her head for me while she's still dazed..."

"Ah…I'm afraid that's not how the divine-help thing works," said Athena. "We give you the basic equipment and some directions, but you have to put in some effort. How else do you expect to become a hero? I mean, we can't do it all for you, can we? That wouldn't really be fair."

"I should have known it wasn't going to be easy," Perseus muttered, disappointed. "Nothing ever is. OK then, what have you got for me?"

"Some excellent stuff, actually," said Athena. "So make sure you pay attention." She wrinkled her nose, and a pair of winged sandals instantly replaced his old ones. "They'll take you to Medusa, and bring you back," said Athena. "Just start running and you'll see…" She wrinkled her nose twice more, and Perseus found himself holding a shield with a mirrored surface, and a sharp sickle. "Use the shield to look at Medusa, and the sickle to cut off her head." Athena wrinkled her nose one last time, and Perseus found he had a large leather bag tied to his belt. "And that's to put it in," she said. "You still shouldn't look at it, even when she's dead. Well, off you go then, young man. Oh, and, er…jolly good luck!"

Athena started shimmering, and Perseus heard the sound of that strange, haunting music again. "Wait, please, Your Wondrousness!" Perseus said desperately. "I wanted to ask…"

But it was too late. Athena vanished, and Perseus was left standing alone in the shade of the ancient olive tree.

"Oh, great," he murmured, although he had begun to feel a definite stirring of excitement at the prospect of adventure. He looked down at the winged sandals on his feet. What had Athena said? Just start running… Perseus gingerly took a step forwards… and felt his foot tingle. So he took another, and another, and then he broke into a run, and suddenly he realised that he had left the ground…and was flying through the air.

"Wow, this is fantastic!" Perseus yelled, but the wind stole the words from his mouth. Below him he could see the whole of Seriphos, and the sparkling, wine-dark waters that surrounded it. Soon he was flying over other islands dotted in the sea like the stars in the night sky, and then he was descending, the winged sandals bringing him to a dry, rocky land, the sun now hidden by grey clouds, the air cold and smelling of sulphur.

His feet touched ground at last, and he stood there for a moment to get his bearings. If Athena had been right about the sandals, then this was the land of the Gorgons, so he would have to be careful. He glanced round cautiously, and seeing some odd-looking figures up ahead, he set off to investigate, keeping himself covered with the shield and the sickle raised.

The figures were very strange. They appeared to be warriors, dozens of them, but none were moving. Perseus studied a few closely, and saw that they were all made of stone, so he decided they must simply be statues.

But they were disturbingly lifelike, everything about them amazingly detailed, right down to the expressions of utter terror on their faces…

Suddenly Perseus felt the hairs stand up on the back of his neck, and the cold hand of fear grip his heart. These weren't statues – they were warriors who had been turned to stone by the terrifying gaze of the Gorgon Medusa! And that meant she was probably somewhere nearby.

"Who comes to the home of Medusa?" a voice growled. "Another hero seeking my head? Well, don't be shy, step forward and gaze upon me…"

From the corner of an eye, Perseus caught a brief glimpse of someone in the distance, beyond the petrified warriors. He ducked down, realising it must be Medusa, and felt terrified that he was about to turn to stone. But he didn't, much to his relief. He still needed to work out exactly where she was, though. So he propped the mirrored shield against the nearest warrior, and angled it so that he could see the Gorgon clearly.

She really was a gruesome, scary sight. Her face was incredibly ugly, the leathery skin a mouldy green, her eyes a vile, sickly yellow, her mouth stuffed with razor-sharp teeth, two big ones sticking up from her wet bottom lip like the tusks of a wild boar. Deadly snakes grew out of her head instead of hair, and they writhed and hissed continually.

For a moment, Perseus's courage failed him, and he almost turned and fled. But he got a grip on himself. He had come this far, and he wasn't about to give up. Besides, he had noticed that Medusa wasn't exactly the most mobile of monsters. She seemed to be sitting on a throne in some sort of small temple, and the only part of her that moved was her head. So maybe he could do it after all.

Perseus took a deep breath…then stood up, slung the mirrored shield on his arm and set off towards the Gorgon. He kept the shield angled towards Medusa, and looked down at her reflection in it, never directly at her. She soon saw him coming.

"Ah, there you are!" growled Medusa. "I knew I had company… But what's this? A boy sent to do a man's work… What is the world coming to? And why so bashful, sonny? Don't you want to take a proper peek?"

"Er…not really," murmured Perseus, moving closer and closer, until at last the Gorgon's hideous face almost filled the shield. The snakes were hissing furiously now, and he could hear them snapping at him. He paused, checked the reflection once more and raised the sickle. The snakes suddenly went still, and a troubled expression crept over Medusa's face.

"Hang on a second," she said. "Your name's not…Perseus, is it?"

"It is, actually," said Perseus, a little surprised. "How did you guess?"

"Oh, it was pretty easy," said Medusa, sighing. "I suddenly remembered an old prophecy, that's all, about being killed by a boy called Perseus. And do you know, when I woke up this morning I had the strangest feeling that something awful was going to happen today…"

"Well, you were right," said Perseus. "Sorry!" Then with one swift, clean stroke of the sickle he cut off her head. "Ugh…" he said as he picked it up and popped it into the leather bag, still making sure that he didn't look at it. He tied the top of the bag shut, attached it to his belt once more, and stood there grinning. He had succeeded where all those other great heroes had failed! He couldn't wait to get back to Seriphos.

Before long he was flying high in the sky again, the same panorama of islands and sea whizzing beneath him. He landed at the palace gates and strode past the amazed guard, then headed for the hall. He pushed open the doors, still holding the shield and the sickle, Medusa's blood dripping from it, the drops burning holes in the marble floor where they fell.

It seemed that the king's birthday party wasn't over just yet. Polydectes and his bodyguards and the island's rich boys were stuffing their faces with food and drinking lots of wine – or at least, that's what they'd been doing till Perseus interrupted them. Now everyone was staring at him with their eyes wide and mouths open, which was a disgusting sight.

"I take it you weren't expecting me so soon, Your Majesty," said Perseus. "Or maybe you were hoping I wouldn't be coming back at all."

"I wasn't bothered one way or the other," said the king, recovering his poise. "I was pretty sure you wouldn't do what you promised, although you've probably got some wild story full of lies and excuses. Still, I'd like to know where you got that ridiculous shield. Is it your mother's, perhaps? A family heirloom? Oh, I forgot. Your family has…nothing."

The bodyguards and young men laughed, and Polydectes sneered.

"Actually, I did what you asked of me," Perseus said quietly. "I have Medusa's head here in this bag. What would you like me to do with it?"

"I don't believe it!" snapped Polydectes, his face dark red with anger, his lips flecked with spittle. "You're obviously just making fun of me. Well, I'll show you what it means to incur the wrath of King Polydectes. I'm going to kill you as slowly and painfully as I can. Seize him, men!"

The bodyguards drew their swords and began to advance on Perseus, the rich boys swarming behind them like a pack of eager jackals. Perseus frowned, and turned to leave, but more guards had arrived at the door behind him and his only escape route was blocked. He didn't even have room for a good run so that his sandals would kick into action.

This was the end, he thought. He should have known Polydectes would pull this kind of stunt. He was doomed…but then he had an idea, and he smiled.

"I wasn't making fun of you, Polydectes," he said, untying the bag from his belt. "I do have the head of Medusa, and I can prove it to you."

"Go on, then!" said Polydectes, laughing as he drew his own sword.

"OK, you asked for it," said Perseus. "You might regret it, though…"

He plunged his hand into the bag, pulled out the Gorgon's head, and held it up, keeping his eyes averted from that dreadful sight, of course. Everyone else in the hall looked straight at it, however – the bodyguards, the rich boys, Polydectes himself. There was a brief, collective gasp of total horror – and then they were all instantly transformed into stone.

"Perseus one, Polydectes nil, I think," said Perseus with a grin. He carefully put Medusa's head in the bag, and went home to his mother.

Things certainly improved for them from that day on. Danae did get married eventually – to a good man Perseus liked, who also happened to be rather wealthy. (Zeus didn't come to the wedding, but he did send a nice present.) And Perseus, of course, became a great hero, known throughout the world for his courage and his legendary exploits, and especially for being the boy who tackled the evil Medusa – and lived to tell the tale!

A BOY GOES OUT TO BATTLE
THE STORY OF DAVID AND GOLIATH

ONCE, LONG AGO in the ancient, troubled land of Judea, there was a boy called David. He was the youngest son of Jesse, a farmer who lived in Bethlehem, a small village in the hills. Jesse had eight sons all told, and being the youngest had its problems. David loved his brothers, but to them he was the baby of the family, and they often made fun of him.

At that time, David's people – the Israelites – were at war with the Philistines, a tribe of fierce fighters. One day, news came to Jesse's farm that the Philistines had marched deep into the heart of the Israelites' land, and King Saul had called for men to face them in battle. The future of Judea was at stake, and David's brothers stepped forward to volunteer.

"Hey, count me in too!" said David when he heard what was happening. His job was to look after the family's sheep, and he had just brought the flock in from the hills for the night. "I definitely want to go."

"Don't be stupid," said his oldest brother, Eliab. "It will be men's work, David – proper fighting, not some pretend adventure for a little boy."

"I'm not a little boy," said David. "I'm nearly grown-up, and I'm tired of you lot treating me like a child. You'll let me go, Father, won't you?"

Jesse had always had a soft spot for his youngest son, and sometimes indulged his wishes. But on this occasion Jesse agreed with his firstborn.

"No, I'm sorry, David," he said. "Eliab is right – you're just not old enough to be a warrior. Your day will come. In the meantime, you can help me make sure your brothers have everything they need…"

For a second, David felt like saying no himself, and running off to sulk. But instead he helped his brothers gather their weapons and armour, and load their packhorses with food and drink. They left the next morning, and David took the family's flock back to the hills. Then he sat under a tree and brooded as the animals bleated and nibbled at the juicy grass.

How could he become a man if things carried on this way? His father and brothers never gave him a chance. He hated the thought that while his brothers were going to fight for their people, he would be stuck at home doing nothing more than looking after a bunch of smelly woolly-backs. Although being a shepherd wasn't exactly a child's game. There were often threats to the flock. Why, this winter alone David had fought off jackals, a couple of wolves, and a hungry lion that had come sniffing down the cold wind for prey. He had even had to kill a huge bear.

The creature had attacked at twilight on a misty evening. David had whipped

out his trusty sling, whirled it round his head once, twice, three times, and let fly with one of the special stones he used for ammunition. He had hit the bear in the forehead, and the beast had crashed to the ground like a great tree blasted by lightning. It was only afterwards that David had realised just how close to a grisly death he had come…

Time went past, and no news came. The days turned into weeks, and then one morning a messenger arrived. David's brothers had almost run out of food and drink, and Eliab had sent the messenger to ask Jesse for more. David begged his father to let him take it to them, and Jesse eventually gave in, although he did make David promise to be careful.

David set off, leading a couple of packhorses loaded with food and drink. The next day, he came to the Valley of Elah, the place where the two armies faced each other. David paused on a hill and gazed down.

The army of the Israelites was in a camp on one slope of the valley, and on the opposite slope was the army of the Philistines. Warriors on both sides were warily watching each other, but most were just sitting round their campfires, or sheltering in their tents from the heat of the sun.

It seemed very peculiar. This wasn't what war was like in the stories David's brothers liked to tell. He had expected to see men fighting, and maybe even some blood and gore. But absolutely nothing was happening. David was intrigued, and quickly descended with the packhorses. The camp of the Israelites was very quiet, and David couldn't help noticing that most of the men seemed bored, and even rather miserable.

At last he came to the tents of his brothers. They were sitting round their campfire, not speaking, and looking just as unhappy as the other Israelite warriors. Then Eliab glanced up, saw David, and scowled at him.

"What are you doing here?" he growled. "If you've run away without telling Father, you can go straight home. This is no place for little boys."

"I've brought the supplies you asked for," said David, nodding at the packhorses. "And what's the big deal? I don't see much going on that's dangerous... In fact,

if I didn't know you men were supposed to be fighting against our deadliest enemies I'd think you were on holiday."

Eliab scowled at him more fiercely now, but he didn't disagree, and neither did any of the others. They glanced at each other, their cheeks burning with shame. Even Eliab began to look uncomfortable.

"It's very…complicated," he said at last, and the others nodded in agreement. "Grown-up stuff, too difficult to explain to a kid like you."

"Try me," David murmured. He stood there waiting, arms folded.

So Eliab sighed, and told David what he wanted to know. It turned out that the two armies were evenly matched – neither side had enough men to be sure of defeating the other. So they had settled into an uneasy standoff. For forty days, the Israelites had been unable to make the Philistines leave their land, and the Philistines had been unable to conquer it either.

"What are you going to do, then?" David said. "You can't just sit here waiting for the Philistines to leave. Doesn't the king have any ideas?"

"Who knows what goes through the great king's mind?" muttered Eliab, and the others all rolled their eyes. "Our strange and moody monarch hides in his tent with his priests and his fortune-tellers, hoping for a miracle. But one of the Philistines has been making a suggestion…"

Just then David heard a man start yelling in the distance. Each time the man paused, there was a roar of many voices followed by a CRASH!

"And there he is," Eliab said grimly. "Right on time, as usual. Come on, little brother. I guarantee you won't ever have seen anything like this."

Eliab and the others jumped to their feet and headed off in the direction of the noise. David went after them, and was soon part of a great throng of Israelites emerging from the camp and spreading out on their side of the valley. David pushed through to be at the front with his brothers.

And there before him on the opposite slope was a chilling sight. The Philistines had come out of their camp too, and were lined up for battle, their helmets and shields and the sharp points of their spears glittering in the sunlight. But one Philistine warrior stood in front of the rest.

The Philistine was enormous beyond belief, much taller and broader than any man David had ever seen – a giant, in fact. He was wearing an immense brass helmet and gleaming armour, and carrying a huge sword and a shield the size of a cartwheel.

Suddenly the giant yelled again, his booming voice filling the valley.

"Another day goes past, and I, Goliath the Great, offer you Israelites the same challenge," he called out. "Choose a champion to fight me in single combat!" The Philistines roared, and beat their shields with their spears – CRASH! "Let's put an end to this ridiculous standoff!" yelled Goliath, and there was another great roar and CRASH! "Winner takes all. Your champion wins – we leave. I win – WE RULE JUDEA FOREVER!"

The Philistines roared even more loudly, and yelled insults now too, calling the Israelites cowards and weaklings and other names too vile to mention. David waited for a response from the warriors around him, but none came. The Israelites stood silent, their faces filled with shame.

"What's wrong with everyone?" David said to Eliab. "Why doesn't somebody accept his challenge and shut that big idiot up for good?"

"Because it would be certain death, that's why," snapped Eliab. "Just look at him, David. There isn't a warrior here who could take him on and win. And who wants to be remembered as the man who lost our land?"

There was a murmur of agreement from David's brothers, and other men nearby. David could hear Goliath still yelling, and the Philistine warriors banging their shields and laughing at the Israelites. Suddenly David's young heart grew hard against the warriors around him.

"You call yourselves men?" he said. "Well, I might only be a little boy, big brother, but I can see that Goliath is right in wanting to end all this hanging about. So I'll gladly accept his challenge. I'll be our champion."

"Don't...don't be ridiculous," spluttered Eliab. "You can't fight..."

"Who are you to say what he can't do?" a nearby warrior yelled. "Let him have a go if he wants. Anything is better than this endless waiting!"

Other voices were raised in agreement. Eliab argued with them, and with David, and someone finally said that they should let the king decide. So David was swept off by the mob and taken to the great tent of King Saul. The crowd called for the king to come out, and he did at last. He stood surrounded by his bodyguards and priests and fortune-tellers.

King Saul's dark eyes glittered when he heard what David had said. Silence descended once more on the Israelite warriors as they waited for their king to speak. A priest leaned over to whisper in one royal ear, then a fortune-teller in the other. And eventually… King Saul nodded.

"Perhaps I will have my miracle after all," he murmured. "Prepare the boy for battle. I will allow him to use my weapons and armour."

Once more David was swept forward by the crowd, only this time to be strapped into the king's fine armour. The king's sword was thrust into his hand, and then he was hurried back to the valley slope, a huge crowd of warriors behind him. Somebody shoved him out into the open ground, and he stood squinting in the sun, the king's helmet heavy on his head.

Goliath was just turning away, but one of the Israelites yelled at him.

"Wait, Goliath!" he said. "Our champion is here to fight you!"

Goliath peered across the valley. David could see him grinning, and the Philistines pointing and nudging each other. Suddenly he felt his cheeks burning.

"Is that the best you can do?" yelled Goliath. "I like the fancy armour, but you should have chosen a man to fight me, not a little boy."

The Philistines roared with laughter now, and David couldn't blame them. Everything had happened so fast since he had volunteered to be the champion that he'd hardly had time to draw breath. He realised now that he must look totally ridiculous. The king's armour was simply too big for him – the helmet kept slipping down over his eyes, the breastplate hung loose from his shoulders and he could barely hold up the great shield.

An argument had broken out in the Israelite ranks, somebody saying that it was a stupid idea, Eliab shouting to David to stop being a fool and risk losing Judea to the Philistines. And suddenly David wondered what he was doing there, a boy standing in a valley between two armies of men, and he was tempted to run away and hide behind his brothers.

But he knew that if he did, he would never be a man even if he grew to be taller than Goliath himself. Everyone would always think of him as the boy who had fled from the Philistine. He would have to fight him, here and now, as he had fought jackals and wolves and that bear. And thinking of how he'd dealt with the bear made David feel he could win… But he had to fight in the only way he knew how.

David threw the sword and shield down with a clatter, then pulled off the helmet and the breastplate and cast them aside too. The Philistines laughed even more when they saw his slight, boyish figure, and Eliab called out again. David ignored him and walked forward, his head high.

He pulled out his sling, loaded it with a stone and kept it behind his back.

"Hey, Goliath!" he yelled, his voice just loud enough to be heard above the catcalls and laughter. "You wanted someone to fight. Well, fight me!"

"Go home, little boy," sneered Goliath, dismissing him with a wave of his huge hand and turning to go once more. "It's way past your bedtime!"

The Philistines jeered and laughed at him, but David kept advancing.

"What's wrong, you big ape?" he shouted. "Frightened I'll beat you?"

Goliath stopped, and swivelled on his heel. He glowered at David, and both armies fell silent. A sudden breeze blew dust round David's feet. He swallowed hard, tightened his grip on his sling and met the giant's gaze.

"I fear no one, man or boy," Goliath growled angrily. He raised his sword, hefted his shield and roared his war cry. "Prepare to die, Israelite!"

Then he came thundering down the valley slope, moving incredibly fast for a big man, the ground trembling as he ran. The Philistines cheered him on, and David heard Eliab yell, "Run for your life, David!"

But it was far too late for that. David ran towards Goliath instead, his eyes fixed on the giant's face, searching for the best spot to aim at. And there it was, a small area of skin between Goliath's eyebrows and his helmet rim.

They were almost in the bottom of the valley now, getting closer and closer to each other. David could feel his heart pounding in his chest, his breath coming in gasps,

but he also felt strangely calm. He whirled his sling once round his head, twice, three times...then let fly, the stone WHOOSHING through the air and SMACKING into Goliath's forehead.

For an instant the giant simply looked surprised. But soon his eyes rolled up into his skull, and – like the bear – he crashed to the ground and lay still. A great gasp of disbelief and dismay came from the Philistines. David slowly walked over and nudged Goliath with his foot to make sure he was quite dead. He stood on the giant's back and held his sling aloft.

Then he roared his triumph to the sky, and his people roared too.

Eliab and his brothers came running out to him, and lifted him onto their shoulders. David smiled as he was acclaimed by the Israelites...

There's not much more to say, except that David's example helped the Israelite warriors find their courage – and the Philistines lose theirs. They were chased out of the valley, and right out of Judea. From then on David was a hero, and in due time he became a king far greater than Saul ever was, one with his own fine armour and weapons. But that's another story.

And he will always be remembered for what he did that day, when he became David – the Boy Who Slew a Giant with a Little Stone!